# To Love You Again

Solara Gordon

Published by THE EARTH MOVED, LLC, 2020.

This is a work of fiction. Similarities to real people, places, or events are entirely coincidental.

TO LOVE YOU AGAIN

**First edition. December 27, 2020.**

ISBN: 978-1733039475

Written by Solara Gordon.

Thank you to the following for their generous help and feedback on Grey and Amie's story: Tom Crepeau (Beta Reader Extraordinaire), Denise Leitch-Gaff, my street team, and readers group 'Solara's Glamorous Stars' and my many author friends who provide insight into the writing and publishing business.

# CHAPTER ONE

Grey Dunstan looked around McGalvin's dining area. Every table and booth was occupied. Several servers greeted him as they walked by. Jonathan hadn't let him down. Grey knew his ex Amie Ferguson waited for him. Jonathan had reserved their usual table. Every Valentine's Day, he and Amie had lunch together. What had started out as support after they're mutual break-up had led to best friends and confidantes. Grey shielded his eyes knowing that Amie was probably not watching for him. She'd be reading an e-book on her phone. There was a time when his jealousy of her e-books and seeking solitude swamped him. Caused him to lay down a mandate that started their break up. Now he knew that was Amie. She worked long hours, sometimes double shifts at the hospital. His brash youthful self had matured.

He moved forward into the dining area toward the back section close to the kitchen. A small two-person booth close to the kitchen door was theirs for the next couple of hours. As he sidestepped around a server carrying a tray laden with orders, he saw her. Amie looked up, smiled, and waved. She slipped her phone into her purse as he approached. This was a change.

Amie rubbed her lips together as she sighted Grey. His hair was grayer, more salt and pepper than last year's. Her auburn locks were graying too. Each of them had weathered more than their share of life's ups and downs. Neither of them had shied away from their conversations or rants and raves when they needed them. Grey was someone she trusted. Someone who knew about most of the skeletons in her past and current life. He was more than a best

1

friend or just an ex or old boyfriend. He was another part of her life just as she possibly was his. Was she?

Grey slid into the seat opposite her. "Hi. Same time. Same place."

Amie laughed. "Sure is. Good to see you." She laid her hand palm up on the table.

"Good to see you too. I thought I might have to cancel." Grey looked down. She hoped he was noticing her hand and not looking at the menu in front of him.

"I'm glad you didn't. Why would you have cancelled?" Amie watched Grey place his hand on the table not far from hers.

"Sandy called. You remember her. My step-daughter by my second marriage." Grey leaned forward causing his hand to slide closer to hers.

"Yes, she married my cousin Sheila's son Brook. How are they doing?"

"Up and down. Fight like two pissed off chickens to quote Sandy." Grey laughed. "She called to tell me she's pregnant."

Amie rocked back. "Pregnant? How did...damn, I know how that happened." She chuckled.

"Glad you do. Means I don't have to waste time explaining that to you." Grey's smile always lit up his face to the point even his eyes glowed. Another part of her caught the glow too. Now if her mind would stay on the conversation and not on what her hormones were signaling they wanted to do with Grey, she'd get through this lunch without having to fan herself.

"Not right now for sure. How are Sandy and Brook handling their news?"

"Pretty well. Sandy is gathering ideas for names. Brook is trying to decide if he likes Poppa or Daddy better." Grey pulled his hand back.

Amie slid hers back too. She dropped her hand into her lap, glad Grey hadn't discovered her sweaty palm. She wiped both hands down her jeans. "I'm happy for them. You gonna be a grandpa?"

"More of an adopted one. Sandy always felt closer to me than her estranged father. She introduces me as her adopted dad. Her mother gave up on correcting her a while back. So getting used to Grandpa is going to take a bit." Grey picked up his menu.

Amie nodded. "What are we going to try this time? Jonathan said he had some new entrees we might like."

Grey looked up, his gaze not leaving hers. "I think food is not what I have in mind."

Amie swallowed hard. What was Grey saying? "Uhm, I thought we were here for lunch."

"Oh, that is part of it. I got a couple things I wanna talk about after we get caught up." Grey went back to looking at the menu.

Amie tried to take a deep breath, calm her fluttering stomach, and concentrate on the menu. Every time she snuck a glance at Grey, he caught her, smiled, nodded, and looked back at the menu. She nibbled her bottom lip with her teeth as she picked up her menu and tried to decide what she wanted to eat.

Grey knew that look, knew when Amie nibbled her lip he'd gotten to her. Maybe even given her wet panties as she used to accuse him of when he passionately French kissed her. He hoped he'd gotten her hot, bothered and made her clit swell. He glanced over the menu one more time. Food wasn't what preoccupied his thoughts. It would have to do for now. Amie needed a chance to bring him up to speed on what was going on in her life. He knew from their past and her ex relationships that being heard and understood mattered to her. He learned firsthand in his last relationship just how important that was. Being cutoff, wants and desires along with needs swept off the table with a disregard for him as a person had stung. Stung so bad, he'd not taken a chance on another date until he crossed January 31$^{st}$ off his calendar and turned the page to February 1$^{st}$. Almost a year had passed since that break up. Time for hiding and protecting his heart was over.

"I think I'll try the Cordon bleu sandwich with sweet potato fries. Jonathan makes his own five-grain bread." Grey laid his menu on the table. "What are you having?"

Amie looked up. She grinned at him. "It's like Jonathan is serving nouvelle meals with a twist. I'm having the Cajun chicken salad on mixed baby greens with grated gorgonzola cheese and fresh blueberries with a side of the house honey mustard dressing."

Grey held his hand up as one of the servers approached the kitchen. "We're ready to place our orders."

"Very good sir." The server set his tray on a close by empty table. He hasty wrote their order on his pad and confirmed the order. "Anything else to drink besides water?"

"I'm good with that. You, Amie?" Grey asked.

"I'm fine with water."

Grey waited until the server left before he spoke. Amie kept eyeing him as if she expected him to say something wrong. The last time they'd gotten into a rather personal conversation, they'd dropped the topic like it was a hot potato they tossed back and forth. They hadn't spoken to each other for two months that time. He wasn't going to let that happen today or going forward. He knew what he wanted. Getting Amie to talk it out was necessary if they were going to move forward.

He smoothed his napkin across his lap, took a sip of water, swallowed, and cleared his throat. Amie glanced up, her lips pressed together. He hated making her wait, but she needed to know he cared about where her life was and what her focus was. He laid his hands on the table, leaned forward, and said, "I want to hear about what's going on with you. I really do."

Amie toyed with her napkin and utensils before meeting his gaze. "Are you sure?"

"Yes." He took a hold of Amie's hand, entwining his fingers with hers. "You matter. Knowing what's going on with you matters too. It's all part of you."

Amie didn't pull her hand away. Good, she would have previously. Getting her to relax with him was an integral part of their post lunch conversation. Meanwhile, it was her turn to talk.

Amie rubbed her lips together. She glanced at their joined hands. Grey had reached out to her, even touched her without obvious prodding. Heat sizzled off his palm, across her fingertips and down over her palm and wrist until she felt the warmth drip off her, and pool in her lap. It was like it sought her out, reaching out and soaking her in its presence to seep deeper into her igniting a larger flame of desire.

"Well, I-I," she stopped speaking. Damn, her stutter crept up when she got nervous. She inhaled, wet her lips, and started again. "I quit my job at the hospital."

"Why?" Grey asked.

# CHAPTER TWO

Amie waited for Grey to say more. He didn't. She nodded as she started speaking. "It got to be more than what I wanted. Four ten hour shift days or three twelve hour shift days were what was offered me or I could take a promotion into management. One of the charge nurses had retired. No one knew she and I had become good friends. She told me a month before she submitted her notice why she retired."

"What was it? It sounds like over worked and undervalued." Grey let go of her hand.

"Yes, very overworked and under paid too. The promotion only offered a four to five thousand raise. Charlotte told me follow my gut and heart. I decided it was time to work for me. I opened up a crafts shop down on Main and Fourth near the Colonial Times museum and the Artists' Loft warehouse." Amie settled back against her seat. She counted to ten, watching Grey, waiting for his reaction.

Grey smiled and nodded. "Good area. How long have you been open?"

"A couple of months. Business is starting to pick up. The local art and craft shows are bringing in new clients." Amie slowly exhaled and relaxed into the booth's seat. She'd found her love of knitting and needle point fed her artist side in ways, paints and canvass ignited her business partner's love of art history and sponsoring young budding artists showcases at the warehouse. "Here's the added bonus, Charlotte bought into the business and is helping out with her connections to the warehouse and her art history knowledge."

"I like the enthusiasm in your voice. Your energy too. Congrats on finding part of what makes you *juicy*." Grey's emphasis on juicy got her hormones' juice going even stronger.

"Thank you." Amie let go a deep sigh. She reached across the table, her palm up again. "I need your help with something."

Grey didn't hesitate. He laid his palm on top of hers. Heat, followed by pinpricks across her palm and fingertips, seared its way around her wrist and encircling her forearm up to her elbow. Amie tried to take a breath. Heat enveloped her until she thought she'd start sweating.

Grey cupped his hand around hers, squeezed, and drew his hand back. "I'll help you as best I can. How can I help you?"

Amie looked down and back up catching Grey watching her intently like he had since he'd sat down. He was paying attention, close attention to what she said, and trying to read her body language at the same time. This was very different. That along with his saying he'd do his best to help her. Previously, he'd wish her luck and offer the names and phone numbers of people who could help her. What was going on?

She inhaled, slowly exhaled, and said, "I need a place to stay. Rent or maybe buy. Living in the backroom of the shop isn't working." She'd put it out there. There was no turning back now.

Grey pressed his lips together knowing if he blurted out his response, Amie would think he was mocking her. He'd done that in the past. They'd worked out a truce and understanding he'd honored for the last four years. Today he wanted to tell her she had a home, a place where she could stay as long as she wanted. A place he hoped she never left. He waited a couple of more moments. "Okay," he began as their server came up to the table with their orders.

Five minutes passed, very tightly filled with silence minutes. As soon as their server left, Grey leaned forward as far as he could without diving across the table. He laid his arm on the table between their plates of food and placed his hand on Amie's arm as best he could. "Let me get this out here and now. I know a place you can stay as long as you want. Details can be worked out."

"You do? Where?" Amie put her hand on his. She'd touched him without hesitation. This might work.

"With me." Grey didn't wait for her response before adding. "I bought a four bedroom house on Bay Street last year. There's plenty of room for both of us."

Amie pulled her hand off his, looked away, and back at him. Her gaze met his for a few moments before she looked away again. Grey slowly leaned back, removing his arm from the table. Learning how to read body language served him well. His time in therapy had taught him many things. One of the best was focusing outward when someone got quiet. Actively listening with an empathic focus hadn't come easy. He'd worked through a bunch of crap to get to a point where he could keep quiet and give the silent person time to regroup or speak.

Grey cut his sandwich in to quarters, laid his knife aside, and studied Amie for a few moments. She still refused to look at him. She busied herself with her salad and mixing it with the honey mustard dressing. Next, she cut up the salad and chicken chunks several times. If, she kept dicing and slicing, there wasn't going to be any salad left. It was going to be diced-and-sliced chopped bits. What he'd said had gotten to her. But, how and why. He'd give her a few more moments then he was going to say something.

Amie closed her eyes, slowly inhaled and exhaled. She felt every staccato beat of her heart every time she peered at Grey through her eyelashes. He'd said the one thing she hadn't expected. Share a place with him. Live with him. They'd lived together once. Even jumped over the proverbial broomstick twice, once as a renewal ceremony. Somewhere within their second ten years together, they messed up super bad. Mucked it up good as her Granny used to say. Except she knew Grey's summation of fucking things up horribly explained the whole episode better than she could have. Over the last four years, they'd agreed that the past was done and over with. Early on in the years right after their break up, they'd avoided each other. What was going to make this time any different? Shit, she didn't want to lose her best friend. She liked knowing Grey was around. There when she needed him.

She stabbed her salad, raised a fork full, and raised her head. Grey watched her. He saluted her with part of his sandwich, took a bite, and chewed. Christ, was this another of his cat and mouse games? Well, she wasn't going to let him corner her. Not that he had since their break up. Still she felt she knew what he would do next—Or did she?

Amie laid her fork full of salad on her plate. She gripped her napkin in one hand. Grey couldn't see what she was doing with the table between them. She waited until he wiped his mouth before she spoke. As he reached for his glass, she asked, "Are you sure? Last time we tried this...well, I don't want to put our friendship at stake."

Grey's grin reminded her of the Cheshire cat from the Alice in Wonderland film she recently watched with her six-year-old great niece. He winked at her and said, "Yes, I'm sure. Very sure. This time we've got a whole house to get lost in. Not like that studio apartment we ended up in when I lost my job."

Amie nodded picked up her fork and started eating. Her stomach had growled twice while she decimated her salad. What a mess she'd made of it. Now it was time to eat it and ponder her next move.

Grey finished the last quarter of his sandwich. He reached for another sweet potato fry when Amie pointed her fork at him. She'd done that before. It was like she punctuated emphatically what she said. She motioned with her hands when she felt threatened. What was it about moving in with him that appeared to unnerve her? A two-story house, her own room and bath. Damn, she'd have her own key, a place in the garage to park her second hand SUV. It wasn't like he'd put conditions on it. He hadn't said a word about rent. What had her riled up?

# CHAPTER THREE

"What's got you stirred up?" Grey asked, tossing his napkin on his empty plate. "I'm not making assumptions. Please explain why you're agitated about my offer."

Amie ate another fork full of salad, slowly chewed and drank some water. "I'm not riled. I'm concerned is all."

Grey leaned back, counting to ten as he did. He knew his expectations. Amie didn't. Another of their prior sticking points. He learned to keep his lip zipped to quote his counselor when giving the other person room to speak. He motioned for Amie to go on.

"What are people going to think? You know?"

"No, I don't know. I'll tell you why I don't know. Because I don't care." Grey picked up his water glass. "How long have we been meeting here every Valentine's Day for lunch?"

"Almost five years," Amie said.

"Right. Has anyone said something to us? Have you heard gossip? Have our friends or family tried to talk us out of this?" Grey drank the rest of his water and set the glass on the table. "I'd like an answer please."

Amie shrugged. She held up her hands and said, "All right. You've got a point. Let me finish my salad. Do you have time to go to Hoopers' for their Red Velvet Cake frozen yogurt? My treat."

"I do. I'd like to talk more about this. I'm serious about my offer." Grey laid his hand palm up on the table.

Amie nodded, leaned forward, and laid her hand—palm down—on top of his. Warmth flashed between them and faded as Amie started to pull her hand away. Grey waited a few moments until his palm cooled more before he removed his hand. A spark happened, more than once. Had Amie felt it too?

Each time they'd touched, chemistry happened. Heat flowed through and over them. If palm-to-palm they were like this, what would happen if they were nude? Grey glanced at Amie. She attacked her salad like she or it was possessed. He doubted her focus was on food. A memory came to mind. He pressed his lips together lest he start grinning. Amie in lingerie talking about how she didn't look good in it. It had taken him going down on her twice and two hard orgasms before she stopped her lament. He gave up suppressing his grin as one of his favorite memories flashed across his psyche. Amie in black and red silk crotchless panties as she lay on her back, spread eagle, blissed out from the orgasmic pleasure he'd given her. He'd love to do that again and again. Amie willing of course. He wasn't a grab, get what he wanted, and leave his partner unsatisfied. Her pleasure ramped up his pleasure, getting him hotter and harder. If he didn't change his thoughts real quick, his intention was going to tent his pants and give away where his mind wandered. Grey blinked as his focus cleared and his thoughts cooled. Amie watched him intently, almost like a hawk determining if he swooped down on his intended prey.

Amie knew that look. The one that ignited a spark deep in Grey's midsection close to his crotch. The place where he stored his itty-bitty brain he told her one time. Truth was, most men refused to admit they thought about sex often. She did too. Where men got the idea that women didn't enjoy sex as much as men she didn't get. She knew both men and women who rarely gave sex much thought past forty-five. To quote her gynecologist, when her female hormone production started dropping off and menopause began, male hormones got her brain and pussy wet. Wet with excitement and boy could they howl. Some of her dreams leading up to today were filled with flashback memories of her and Grey as lovers. Her early morning dreams the last few days took on a different feel and rhythm. She remembered waking up and reaching across the bed only to find that Grey was a dream figment. Had his hormones turned more feminine? His reason for checking in with her and wanting to talk more about her moving in with him. Did she admit the idea intrigued her? Peaked her interest and got her juicy and wet? Ah well, the discussion hadn't gone that far. Talk about jumping to conclusions. Or was she?

Amie pulled her jacket on and wrapped her scarf around her neck as she stood. The afternoon sun was beginning to wane. She wanted to be back at the shop before the sunset. Her clerk, Roberta, didn't live far from the shop. She didn't like walking home after dark. Her husband was out of town and her son had pulled the late shift at the hospital. Amie faced Grey. "We can go by Hoopers—and get take out if you don't mind? I want to get back to the shop before dark."

Grey nodded. "I can drive you back. I drove into town today."

"Understood. If we get take out, we can sit on the small patio I've got at the rear of the shop and talk more." Amie slung her purse strap over her shoulder.

Grey stood. "Sure, if you don't mind more of my company and talking about my offer."

"That's why I offered. We need to discuss this." Amie stepped away from the table looking over her shoulder.

Grey was putting on his jacket. He moved up beside her, holding the check from their lunch. "My turn to buy, if I remember."

"Yes, that's why I offered to pay for Hoopers. My turn to pay for dessert." Amie smiled and pointed at the check. "Unless you want to split it."

"Nah," Grey replied. "Been working steady. Freelancing is paying off. I consulted two projects for the Midtown Art Gallery. Finally putting my accounting degree to work along with teaching a couple classes at the junior college. Being a CPA has its advantages."

"Maybe you should ask Charlotte out." Amie began making her way through the dining area.

Close to the front, she paused, waiting for Grey to catch up with her. As Grey caught up with her, he took a hold of her hand. "Charlotte might be great to talk art with now and then. I'm not looking for just that. You got a lot of what I'm looking for."

"You what?" Amie stumbled trying to keep up with Grey and wrap her head around what he'd just said.

"I keep coming to lunch because I'm interested in you. You know—friends." Grey stopped by the cash register. "I'll explain when we're in the car."

"Okay," she muttered, unsure how to respond.

Grey usually spoke his peace in such a way she never had to second-guess what he was saying. Now she was trying to translate his intent and read between the lines at the same time. Great and what if she fucked it up? Fouling up was okay—to a point. Grey's wink and quick grin after he said she had a lot of what he was looking for got a reaction. One that sent hot flashes coursing through and over her. It wasn't like she hadn't had a few good orgasms lately. Her toys took care of things rather well. Errr-she took care of things pretty good on her own. It had been a bit lonely and less fulfilling.

Grey glanced over his shoulder. Amie's furled brow and squint told him more than if he'd kept on talking. He'd ignited a spark. It had set off another and another apparently. He knew that look.

Through trial and error over the years, he got what her body language said. Oh, man what her next reaction might be he wasn't guessing. He hoped his explanation kept on fertilizing her imagination and she accepted his offer to make those thoughts and dreams come true.

He tucked the credit card receipt in his wallet and shoved it in his jeans pocket. Amie hadn't moved. It was time to take the lead for the next few moments. He'd explain once they were in the car. He was glad he'd parked on the street instead of the nearby parking garage.

"Let's get out of here," he said, taking a hold of Amie's hand. "What I've got to say is for our ears only."

Amie looked up at him, smiled, and said, "Lord, are you going to whisper X-rated sweet nothings in my ears?"

Grey chuckled. "Could be. Maybe. Come with me and I'll be sure to make your ears, breasts and clit sizzle."

# CHAPTER FOUR

Amie shielded her eyes as she and Grey exited McGalvins. The late afternoon sun warmed the air slightly taking the chill off the breeze blowing in off the lakefront. A light dusting of snow had fallen as they ate, mixing with the tulips and other early spring blooms peeking out in the various window gardens many of the downtown merchants had. Neither of them had their gloves on. Holding hands as they walked brought back memories of her and Grey's early dates. Dates where a shared meal and a shared sundae at Hoopers was the highlight of their week. Weeks often spent working long hours and spending time apart.

Here they were walking down the same street they'd walked before. It didn't seem like years had passed. They had. They weren't trying to make up after arguing or humoring each other because they were over-tired and over-worked. Amie pulled her sunglasses out of her purse and slipped them on. "How far away is your car?"

"About half a block more. Hoopers is three blocks away. Thanks to rush hour traffic starting, its six blocks in the opposite direction." Grey pointed at the no parking sign as he continued. "Good thing we decided to do lunch earlier. Or I'd have a ticket decorating my windshield."

"That fine is hefty too. Don't ask me how I know." Amie grinned and shook her head no twice as Grey opened his mouth. "I said don't ask."

Grey motioned like he was zipping his lips closed and tugged on Amie's hand. She moved closer to him. He slipped an arm around her waist hugging her briefly as they waited for the traffic signal to change to walk. "Subject change, okay?"

"Sure. Go for it." Amie moved away from him as the light changed.

He would have preferred to stay with his arm around her waist. She felt so good there up against him, smiling, and bantering with him. Alas, the light changed and three other people sauntered past them.

"My car is the red sedan. Third one up." Grey fished his keys out of his jacket pocket.

"Red? Wow, I never thought of you with a red car. You always said silver or black were more masculine." Amie stopped close to the car.

"Well, money and gas are the prime decision makers." Grey unlocked the passenger door and opened it. "Repair bills for high-end sportsters is great when you have a hundred thousand a year salary. I also like knowing my car is where I parked it. Not out providing a carjacker a joy ride before it's totaled in an accident or chopped up for parts."

Amie leaned in, brushed her lips across his cheek as she got in the car. "You're so right. Like that not quite vintage car you bought in between jobs. Two hundred thousand miles plus, and they crashed the thing trying to get away from the cops."

Grey snickered. "Hold that thought while I get in."

He stepped off the curb, looked both ways, and scooted around the driver's side of the car. As he got in, he glanced at Amie. She was still smiling. She winked and turned away as she fastened her seatbelt. Five minutes later, he pulled out into traffic knowing the one way flow would take them past Hoopers until they could loop back around on a back street to get into the rear parking lot.

"Thanks for the kiss on the cheek," Grey said merging with traffic. "One of the best Valentine's Day gifts I've gotten in sometime."

"You're welcome." Amie slightly turned toward him. "Looks like it's going to take a while to get to Hoopers."

"Sure does. Gives us time to talk." Grey pointed at the store they were passing. "Isn't that where Robards used to be? Been a while since I noticed what's on this end of Main Street."

Amie laughed. "True. You usually come in from the other direction. Living in the suburbs does that. I had to relearn the neighborhood too once I opened the shop."

Grey grinned and nodded. "Change happens and it can be for the best. We've changed."

"Oh?" Amie asked, looking straight ahead.

Grey wet his lips, considered his response and word choices. How Amie took what he said next might make or break their conversation. "Yes, I don't mean older either. I'm talking about we've changed parts of who we are. Who we were and even who we want to be. Make sense?"

"Some." Amie didn't look at him. With traffic moving slower than a snail, he could let his gaze linger on her or not. People kept j-walking in front of cars.

"I used to think status was based on what I had and my job. How much money I made and who I hung out with." Grey changed lanes as he continued speaking. "Boy did I find out that was wrong."

"How did you?"

Grey chuckled. "Lost a job even though I chummed around with the CEO of the company. People who I thought were friends were acquaintances. A few that stayed in contact helped me out with references and networking options. When I lost the house and car because I couldn't afford them, a few more folks stopped coming around. The ones that did like me and a few other close friends that stuck around showed me through example that money, job, and things weren't what mattered."

"You never let on about this. Why?" Amie glanced at him.

"Because it humbled me. I was ashamed, broken down, and thought that people pitied me. I found out that friends are those who stick by you."

"True. I used to envy your prestige and influential job positions. That's one reason I didn't stay in contact as much for a while. When Sheila asked me about Sandy and started quizzing me about you, I knew I had to make a decision on what was acceptable." Amie shrugged.

"What did you decide?" Grey put on the left turn signal and pulled into the Hoopers back parking lot.

"I valued our friendship. I liked what we'd become—best friends. Someone I could talk to about anything and everything. Even sex." Amie looked at him and grinned. "Now how about I get you juicy and smoldering?"

Grey smirked. "I think we both already are. We've shared some passionate hugs and kisses from time to time. Our chemistry has never dulled. Are we ready for friends with benefits again?"

"*Grey, you are naughty.* That wasn't the topic." Amie looked at her watch. "Instead of eating here, how about I get a quart and we split it at my place? Roberta doesn't like walking home in the dark."

"Sounds good. Go on. I'll wait in the car. There's a parking space close to the door." He stopped close to the Hoopers' entrance. As Amie got out, he added, "Be sure to ask them for a couple of their waffle cups and spoons."

"Sure will." Amie closed the door and walked into Hoopers.

Grey watched Amie for a few moments as he pulled into the parking space he had pointed out. Amie's reply hit him in a couple of ways. They were talking about benefits of being friends and alluding to sex. Why was his question out of place? Maybe. He gripped the steering wheel hard, closed his eyes, and pondered how he'd apologize when Amie got back. He didn't want to start an argument. How did he communicate his interest and not come across as crass? Words could be tricky. Plain clear-cut communication wasn't easy when it was supposed to be.

He looked up as Amie approached the car. She carried two bags and grinned. Grey chuckled. He bet Ella, Mack Hooper's wife, worked the counter. She always gave her favorite regular customers extra goodies. He rolled down his window, holding out a hand. "I can take those. Looks like we got extras."

Amie handed Grey both bags. "Oh, yeah. Ella bagged the last of some goodies for us. She said to tell you stop being a stranger and come by more often."

Grey snorted. "Like either of us gets here more than a couple times a year."

"True. If you make a right, two blocks down is Twinbrook which dead ends in the alley behind my shop. You can park there." Amie pointed to the left hand side of the alley.

"I've got an idea." Grey pulled into traffic. "It's Friday evening. Are you open weekends?"

"Usually. This is my weekend off. I'm supposed to go apartment hunting."

Grey faced her as he put the car in park. "Why don't you pack up a few things and come spend the weekend with me?"

# CHAPTER FIVE

"*What?*" Amie pressed her lips tightly together. More words and stammers wanted to spill out. She knew if she kept talking, she wouldn't make sense. At least, not to anyone other than herself. Coherent conversation halted a few thoughts back.

"I'm asking you to spend the weekend with me. You can check out the house." Grey unfastened his seatbelt and faced her. "There's several apartment complexes in the neighborhoods near me. We can check those out if you feel the need to."

Amie slowly unclenched her hands, smoothed them down her jeans as she forced her thoughts to focus. She'd asked Grey for help. He was offering help. Help in two distinct ways. She'd planned and decided to make her decision on which place quickly. Now she had two offers to consider. One was a sure thing if she took Grey up on his offer. Finding an apartment. . .well that meant applying, deposits, and waiting. Privacy and having a distinct separation between work and home was her top priority. Grey's offer, spending the weekend and sharing his place, aka living together, made sense. Could she calmly talk this out and understand why her hands were sweaty and her stomach wasn't protesting? Talk about mixed reactions.

Grey leaned toward her, holding out his hand. "Look I'm not trying to pressure you into doing this. It's your call."

Amie nodded as she held up one finger. She needed a moment to catch her breath. Spending more time with Grey was something she'd thought about more than once. Did she pinch herself to make sure this was reality?

Grey started to pull his hand back as Amie spoke. He hesitated.

"I think spending the weekend is awesome." Amie lowered her hand. "Caught me off guard. Sorry if I sound leery."

Grey smiled. "Thanks for clarifying that. Had me wondering if I fucked things up twice."

"Fucked up? How?" Amie took his hand. "I thought I was the one messing up."

Grey raised their hands, brushed his lips along Amie's knuckles, his gaze never leaving hers. As he lowered their hands, he spoke. "Guess we both did. Let's agree we'll ask, instead of assuming going forward."

Amie gripped his hand tighter, leaned toward him, whispering, "Yes, talking and asking questions makes sense. Communicate. Communicate more."

"Yup, it sure is about communication. That's another reason I asked you to spend the weekend with me." Grey let go of Amie's hand. "Let's go get Roberta on her way."

Amie grabbed his hand and kissed it. "I'd kiss your lips if you were closer."

Grey opened the car door, got out and leaned back in. "There'll be time for that once we get home."

He straightened, closed the door, and walked around the front of the car, looking up. The sun slipped lower in the sky in the few minutes they had talked. If Roberta was going to get home before dusk, Amie needed to get out of the car.

Sounds of the passenger door closing sounded. Grey pressed his lips together. He knew Amie wouldn't say more until Roberta was on her way home. He watched and waited as Amie made her way up the side of the car. She watched him too. Christ, he wished he was better at reading body language. Uncertainty was a prickly situation. *What are you uncertain about?* his ego spat at him. If he knew, he wouldn't be uncertain.

Amie wondered as she got out of the car if either of them understood where they were going with their banter and what they said. Yet, she knew Grey wasn't teasing. His usual upbeat tone wasn't exactly gone. Neither was it completely noticeable unless she paid close attention. Clutching both Hoopers' bags in her left hand, she dug her keys out of her purse with her right. Priority was getting Roberta on her way home. Maybe Grey would run Roberta home giving Amie a few minutes to gather her thoughts. *Admit you really want to spend the weekend with him? Go home with him?* her subconscious prodded.

Amie handed Grey the bags as they neared the rear entrance of her shop. She turned back toward the door and stopped. "Hello Roberta. Sorry we're running a bit late. Traffic."

The older woman smiled as she exited the building. "No problem. My son called and offered me a ride home."

"Good," Grey said, holding out his hand. "I'm Grey. You must be Roberta. Glad to meet you."

"Yes, I'm Roberta. Amie must have been talking about me again." Roberta laughed and added. "Not that that is a bad thing. I'm glad to meet you, Grey."

Amie faced both of them. "Roberta, I talk about you because you're an asset to my shop. You know about crafting like Charlotte knows about painting."

"Thank you. You let me talk about my passion. My joy and interest. I'm making money at what was my hobby for years. Now I teach people younger than me and my age how to enjoy taking time to sit back and focus on one thing at a time." Roberta zipped her jacket closed and stepped off the small step near the door.

Grey moved sideways to give Roberta room to step off the remaining step as a car turned down the alley. Roberta waived as she stepped off the last step. "That's Talbot, my son. I'll see you Monday, Amie. Have a good weekend, you two."

Grey stood next to Amie as they watch Roberta get in the car after waving a second time. He waited until the car's taillights vanished from view as it turned back on to Twinbrook to face Amie. She glanced at him, shrugged, and moved up the two steps. She spoke before she entered the open doorway. "Come on in. I think I'm ready to give you my decision."

Grey rubbed his lips together. Amie's tone wasn't flat. Nor expressive either. Talk about leaving him guessing. Hell, she was either going to say yes, no or maybe. He could stand on the two-step porch trying to guess her answer or go inside and find out. Grey wiped his feet on the doormat, entered the shop; closing the door behind him. Where they went next, Amie knew. He took two quick breaths, shut the door, and followed Amie into her shop.

Amie paused part way down the hall close to an open door. "This is my office. The next opening goes into the shop. The door at the end of the hall marked private is my studio apartment living space formerly known as the storage room."

"Where are you keeping extra stock? Please tell me you're not sleeping amongst crates and pallets of items." Grey stepped past Amie.

"Stock is limited to what's on hand at the moment. Requests for specialty items have grown as has in house items." Amie faced him. "That is another reason I need to find a place. I need to turn the storage room into a stock room."

"You said you had an answer for me." Grey held up the Hoopers bags. "Wanna tell me over a chocolate dipped waffle bowl with filled with red velvet cake frozen yogurt?"

"Don't forget the rainbow sprinkles and heart-shaped cookies." Amie grinned. "Head on back. The kitchen is on your left as you enter. I'll be there in a moment. I want to make sure Roberta locked up."

Grey started down the hall and turned back. "She'd forget to do that?"

"No. She's very good about it. Has to do with the time my house got broken into while on vacation. Remember?"

"Oh yeah. You called me to come sit with you while the police made their report. I don't blame you. Double checking gives you piece of mind." He stepped back where he could see out into the shop. "I'll wait right here. I want to know you're safe and the shop is locked up tight."

Amie grabbed his hand, squeezed it, and leaned toward him until their lips were very close. She puckered, brushed her lips over his quickly, and pulled back. "Thank you! I really appreciate that."

Amie rushed into the shop, looked behind the counter. The computer was off. The slow steady blink of the front door alarm light greeted her as she moved toward the front door. She checked the first deadbolt lock. Then the second lock. Both lock buttons were turned parallel to the floor. She took a hold of the door handle and pulled. It didn't move. The shop was locked up tight.

As she started back toward the rear of the shop, she moved slower. Knowing Grey waited for her put some of her angst to rest. She still had many questions and knew some answers weren't coming soon.

# CHAPTER SIX

"Everything okay?" Grey moved back into the hall to allow Amie to enter.

"Yes. Front alarm system is on and both locks are locked. Let's go have our dessert and talk." Amie moved past him, continuing down the hall.

There wasn't any hesitation in her answer. No quiver in her voice. It was like she knew her answer and would give it to him when she was ready.

Grey gripped the bags tighter as his ego blipped trying to edge its voice to the top of the heap of feelings bubbling through him. Could he handle another let down? A no given where he was coming into today. *You're mind made up how things were going to turn out, eh?* Great his ego was playing hurt and wounded. He let go a silent sigh, shook his head, and rolled his shoulders. Amie had a say in this and he was going to hear her out. Even talk things out as necessary.

"Sure," he managed to get out, keeping his voice even keeled.

As they got closer to the entrance to Amie's living space, she faced him. "Close your eyes for a moment."

"Huh?"

"Bright lights coming. Overhead light going on in three, two..."

"Wait, please." Grey closed his eyes. "Okay one and go."

Amie's soft laugh reached him. Its warm huskiness wrapped around him like a warm hug and quickly evaporated.

Bright yellows filled the area behind his closed eyes for a moment he was with Amie again watching the sunrise over a white sand beach on the big island of Hawaii. They'd gone there to celebrate their mutual fortieth birthdays. Even though the dates were actually months apart, they both agreed that year to do something either of them had put off and wanted to do before they faced making a bucket list. The squawks and trills of sea gulls sound in the distance part of his memories. Their passion during their week there brought them closer and taught each of them they were best friends. Now could he explain they'd grown beyond that? Could he put his deep intense feelings into words, not just actions?

"Go ahead and open your eyes." Amie took a hold of his hand. "You may need to blink a few times. The overhead light is bright."

Grey squinted, barely opening either eye. The more Amie came into view with each blink, the wider he opened each eye. When he could see her without an overwhelming urge to shield his eyes, he knew he was fine. "Hey beautiful. Love the halo effect."

Amie ducked her head, tittered, and said, "Not bad looking yourself. Rather studly."

Grey nodded, trying to suppress his mirth. They were bantering and making small flirting passes with their words and actions again. May be he was going to be pleasantly surprised.

"Come on." Amie opened the door to her living area. "Please enter my humble temporary abode."

Grey hesitated as he reached the edge of the doorway. Amie's gaze met his. She was smiling and nodding. He grinned, nodded, and moved past her. Two more steps and a low growl sounded. Scampering of feet followed. Grey opened his mouth to ask WTF that sound was. He didn't get a chance to say anything before a small brindle colored blur grabbed his pant leg and started shaking it and itself as it growled more. "What the. . .Amie!"

"Pixie let go. Come here." Amie squatted down near him. "Come on girl. I'm here."

The brindle blur stopped, let go of his pant leg, yipped, and ran to Amie. Grey looked down, blinked, shook his head, and started laughing. "Good watch dog. Pixie is it?"

Amie scooped Pixie up and stood. Cuddling her in her arms, Amie petted Pixie as she replied. "Most of the time, yeah. She usually barks and growls or snaps at ankles. That is a first with a pant leg."

Grey held out his hand at a level Pixie could sniff him. She sniffed, growled, sniffed more, and barked. Grey held his hand steady. "Chihuahuas maybe small. You don't turn your back on them. They've got sharp teeth and will break skin. Pixie is a good girl. Keeping you safe."

Amie stepped closer to him. "Pixie is my four legged burglar alarm."

"Give me your hand. Once she sees me touching you she may settle down more." Amie took a hold of Grey's wrist. ""Pixie this is Grey. He's a friend."

A few more growls sounded as Grey and Amie patted Pixie. Then quiet. Amie set Pixie on the floor. "Sorry about that. I didn't think she'd charge you like that when she heard my voice."

"No problem. Mick will probably be all over you sniffing and trying to sit between us until he gets to know you." Grey bent down and stroked Pixie's back. She wagged her tail and leaned against him.

"Mick?" Amie took off her coat and hung it on the coat pegs on the back of the door. She pushed the door shut.

"Yes, my four legged watch dog. Miniature schnauzer. Got him when he was about six months old from a friend who did a rescue on a breeding farm. Mick was sterile and was badly underweight due to neglect."

"OMG! Poor baby!" Amie set a bowl of food down next to Pixie's water dish.

"Yeah. Took a while to get Mick out of the woods health wise. Now he's rambunctious, loves to chase squirrels, the neighbor's cat, and is a handful when strangers are around." Grey took off his coat and hung it on a peg next to Amie's.

Pixie rushed toward the bowl, putting the brakes on as she got tight to it. Her hind end went up in the air as she took her first bite. All four feet settled back on the floor as she continued to eat.

Grey laughed as he sat on a stool next to the kitchen counter. "Enthusiasm. Love a good show of it. Mick used to upend his bowl until he realized he was the only one eating out of it. He's a great companion."

"Go ahead and serve yourself. I need to wash off a couple of spoons." Amie set the waffle bowls on the counter next to the quart of frozen yogurt. She placed a scoop on the counter. "How's Mick going to handle another dog in the house if I take you up on your offer?"

"He'll get used to Pixie. Mick goes to a doggie daycare on the days I work away from home. He's pretty good about sleeping in his dog bed most nights." Grey pulled his cell phone out of his jeans' pocket and scrolled through several pictures until he found the one he wanted. "Then there's this."

He held the phone out to Amie. She took it, looked down at the picture, and snorted. "Out cold on the couch. Stretched out like he owns it."

"Yup. Has the tenacity to growl at me when I tell him get down." Grey chuckled. "He does get down while he fusses and whines about it."

Grey put two scoops of frozen yogurt in to each bowl. "Two scoops okay for you?"

"Yes. Thank you for serving it." Amie turned, holding out two spoons.

Grey took a spoon and picked up his waffle bowl. He turned toward Amie as she sat on the other stool. Holding out his bowl, he said, "Here's to a great Valentine's Day and to our ensuing discussion, yes?"

Amie laid her spoon down, picked up the plastic bag of rainbow sprinkles, and poured some out on to her yogurt. She set the bag down and raised her bowl. "Yes, an awesome Valentine's Day. And to our interesting discussion, starting now."

Grey picked up the bag of sprinkles, put some on his yogurt, and set the bag down. He took a spoonful of yogurt, saluted Amie, and said, "Okay, I'm enjoying my dessert while you talk."

Amie ate two spoons of yogurt and laid her spoon down. "Don't eat too fast. I don't have a lot to say."

"Oh," Grey responded in between bites.

"Yes. You made an offer. A two fold one." Amie nodded as Grey laid his spoon down. "I've thought about it off and on through lunch and our banter on our way to Hoopers. And. . ."Amie didn't say more.

Grey waited, counted, and waited. Amie went back to eating her yogurt. Talk about bait and maybe switch? Either he spoke up or they could sit here waiting for a long time. Amie could be rather stubborn at times. "You know it would be easier if you said what you're thinking."

"Oh I know that." Amie grinned and broke a piece of her waffle bowl off, pointing it at him. "Making my response that much more tantalizing by waiting and pausing just adds. . .well you know that ups the anticipation, doesn't it?"

# CHAPTER SEVEN

Grey inhaled, let out a long sigh, and shook his head. "Oh, that was good. Good come back. You just upped the banter another level."

Amie laughed. "I do have some questions. Mostly logistical ones."

"Ask away," Grey went back to eating his yogurt.

"I think you need to know my answer first."

"All right. I'm listening." Grey scraped the last of his yogurt out of his waffle bowl.

Amie wiped her hands on her napkin, walked over to the trash and tossed it in. She walked back toward him, grinning. She stopped when she got toe to toe with him. She looped an arm around his shoulders, leaned very close and whispered hotly against his ear. "The answer *is yes*."

Grey swallowed hard, turned slightly, and slipped an arm around Amie's waist. His ego could yammer all it wanted. His ID right along with it. Even his psyche could crow and cheer too. His focus was on the woman he dreamt about having in his arms for the better part of a year. She said she'd spend the weekend with him. It might be the best thing that happened to him in a long time.

Grey moved closer to Amie as he slid his other arm around her. She looped her other arm around his neck closing the circle they made. The closer he got, the surer he was that something right and excellent was happening between them. Part of him wanted to ask about moving in, what were her logistic questions and was she ready to start packing. He knew better though. Rushing things didn't create the future his long lonely nights dreamt of. Nor the pictures he allowed his daydreams to paint in those moments when he shut off from the pain of being alone. Tonight wasn't about making long terms certain plans. It was about spending a weekend together and seeing how possible integrating their lives might be. Still he couldn't—nor would he—still the quiet happily joyous beats his mind and heart made.

He brushed his lips across Amie's cheek, over her lips, and her other cheek. He pulled back until he rested his forehead against hers. Only the tick of the wall clock filled the silence enveloping them along with the beats of their hearts quietly speaking to each other. He stared into Amie's eyes for several moments. He kissed her again and raised his head. "Thank you, darling. I hope you *and* Pixie enjoy spending the weekend with Mick and me."

Amie closed her eyes, savoring the feeling of safeness mixed with a bit of satisfaction. Grey had taken a step outside his comfort zone. She could feel and see it in his tone, his facial expressions and the way he moved. Even his word choices. Caution combined with awareness. Was it calculated moves and nuances on his part or him speaking from his heart? Whatever it was she knew that asking about it could detract from the moment, the mood, and the joy being in each other's' arms brought.

She moved back a bit, breaking Grey's concentration. He blinked and started to move back too. She slid her hands down his arms until they rested on his forearms.

"Wait, please. You're fine. Nothing is wrong." Amie tilted her head back. Grey's gaze remained on her.

"Why did you step back?" Grey began to look away.

"Hey," Amie reached up, cupping his face between her hands. "It's okay. I moved back to see you easier. That's all."

Grey snorted and smirked. "Messed up again, didn't I?"

"Nah. You're trying to be perfect. Not easy." Amie leaned in and brushed her lips over Grey's. "We've been here before and you're going on past memories."

"Fuck, yes. Thought I had learned and changed that." Grey sighed. "Sorry."

"No apology needed. You spoke from here." Amie touched his chest close to his heart.

"Yeah. I think you did too." Grey lowered his arms and moved away from Amie. "Before you pack, I want to answer your logistics questions."

"How about I pack and ask questions at the same time?" Amie walked across the small living space on the opposite side of the storage room.

"Sure. I got one first." Grey turned around on the barstool so he faced Amie as she opened a closet door close to where they entered.

"What is it?" Amie reached into the closet and took out an overnight bag.

"Where do you sleep?" Grey pointed over his shoulder. "Kitchen, got it."

He pointed at Amie. "You're in the living room. I suspect that open door way at the back is your bathroom."

"Very astute. Sofa bed. A very lumpy sofa bed is where I toss and turn with a bit of sleep mixed in." Amie set the overnight bag on the counter. "Any more questions?"

Grey chuckled. "No. This reminds me of the miniscule studio apartment I lived in during college. I loved getting into a one bedroom apartment my senior year."

Amie nodded. "One place I looked at close to the hospital when I thought about taking the management promotion was almost this small. The listing said it was a one bedroom. I didn't stay long enough to investigate where that section was."

"You're going to think the house is a mansion after this." Grey stood and stretched. "What can I do to help?"

"Nothing. I'll be ready in a few. My first question is where do I sleep?" Amie stepped into the closet and kept talking. "Second is, is there a yard? Is it fenced? Pixie likes the dog park. I haven't been able to take her this week."

Grey sat back down. He waited until Amie was out of the closet to answer her. "First question, you sleep anywhere you want. You've got three bedrooms to choose from unless you prefer to share mine."

Amie winked at him. "I'll give it some thought. Your answer to question two."

Grey laughed. "Like your answer. Here's my answer for number two. Back yard fenced in. Hot tub and pool combination. Doggie play yard area. Even a small garden patch."

"You hate yard work, but have a garden. Interesting." Amie put the last of her clothes in the overnight bag. "Last question. . ." She paused, pressed her lips together, and held up two fingers. "Got two more questions."

Grey grinned. "Sure. What are they?"

Amie zipped the bag closed and walked past him, asking, "Who's in charge of birth control? Do you snore? I don't remember."

"Uh-what? Snore? How am I supposed to know?" Grey stood up and leaned on the counter. Had he heard Amie correctly? Birth control? Oh, hell. She must be saying more without coming right out and saying it. Dare he ask the question his thoughts were forming?

"Oh, come on. Your second wife or any of your former girlfriends didn't say you did? What about my other question?" Amie put two bowls with Pixie's name on them in a tote bag along with a couple of toys and several cans of dog food.

"I can't say I snore with certainty. You just have to find out for yourself." Grey shook his head. "And about birth control?"

"Yes, birth control. Unless you're planning on more kids. Or should I say any kids." Amie set the tote on the counter next to the overnight bag.

Grey reached up, stroked his chin twice. His mouth wasn't hanging open. Good. Birth control. Well men didn't take pills like women. Rhythm method was probably out since he and Amie were well past menopause age. And...frack he might as well ask. "Uhm—is condoms okay? You latex sensitive?"

"Yes. Yes. And no. Is a pharmacy stop needed on the way to your place?" Amie washed and dried their spoons. As she came back toward the counter, she opened a cupboard. "Pixie is going to need a quick walk before we go."

Grey put on his jacket, zipped it up, and packed up the remaining frozen yogurt, goodies and bag of sprinkles. He put them in the tote on top of Pixie's bowls. His thoughts ran several directions. Amie had caught him off-guard good. As she put Pixie's coat and leash on her, Amie looked at him and said, "One last question, what if I need to stay longer to make up my mind? You know more than just the weekend?"

Grey pressed his lips together tighter. He inhaled and exhaled slowly. Hopes could expand beyond reality and be crushed if things didn't turn out as his dreams had. Amie stood at the end of the counter watching him. She held Pixie's leash in one hand and her jacket in another. Amie deserved an answer. One that was fair to both of them. How far outside his comfort zone, was he willing to go to do that? "Let's talk while we walk Pixie."

# CHAPTER EIGHT

"Please hold Pixie for a moment while I put my jacket on. She'll dart out the door the minute I open it." Amie held out the end of Pixie's leash. Grey took it.

Amie quickly slipped on her jacket and zipped it up while watching Grey with Pixie. He held her in the crook of his arm, petting her and talking softly to her.

"What a pretty girl. You take good care of your mama. Keep her safe and secure." Grey stroked Pixie's head twice before he looked up. "Ready to go?"

"Yes, thank you. There's a small park down at the end of the next cul-de-sac. By the time we get there, she'll be ready to do piddle and poo. Then back we come. It's about a fifteen minute walk to and from." Amie reached out for Pixie.

Grey started toward the door. "I got her. Grab your bag and the tote. We'll put them in the car. You going to need anything else?"

"I'm good to go." Amie slung her purse strap over her shoulder and stuffed her keys in her jacket pocket. She picked up the overnight bag in one hand, the tote in her other. She waited until Grey was out in the hall before taking one last glance around. Mixed emotions taunted her. She'd gotten used to spending Friday nights binge-watching TV reruns on her laptop computer. She wasn't taking her computer with her. Her latest embroidery project sat in its basket next to the couch. The two items she had quickly picked up off the closet shelf as she packed was a historical romance she'd been wanting to read and a ball of crochet thread, a crochet hook and the accompanying pattern for a doily her sister asked her to make. Grey might need space and she was ready to give him space by keeping herself occupied with either the book or crochet work.

Grey went out the shop's rear entrance first, still holding Pixie. "You lock up. I'll unlock my car. Pixie and I will meet you there."

"Sounds good." Amie turned toward the door, adding. "You can put Pixie down. Just keep a hold of the leash."

Grey grinned as he shifted Pixie from one arm to another. Her feather lightweight was nothing compared to Mick's compact ten muscular pounds. Grey was sure he had doggie kisses on two-thirds of his face. He was glad he had a canister of moist hand wipes in the car.

"All right little one. Down you go. Behave yourself and stay put. You do know how to sit, right?" Grey slipped his hand through the open loop of the leash and gripped the lead in his hand. He patted his jacket pockets with his free hand until he heard the jingle of his keys. Pixie stood up, wagging her tail as he unlocked the car.

"She loves riding in the car." Amie came up behind him.

Grey glanced over his shoulder. "Piddle and poo first. No messes in your chariot Miss Pixie."

Amie grinned, walked around the passenger side of the car, and opened the rear door. "That's why we're taking a walk first. Down to the end of the alley and turn to the left. The cul-du-sac is another block down."

Grey locked the car after Amie put the night bag and tote in the car. "Easy short walk and back to get on our way."

Amie held out her hand. "I can take Pixie's leash."

"She's fine. You lead the way and we'll follow. Right, Pixie?" Grey leaned down and petted Pixie.

Amie stepped away from the car, glancing behind her. Pixie followed with Grey following her. He had a tense grip on the leash. Amie pressed her lips together. Pixie's bursts of energetic running could happen at any moment especially if a squirrel or bird caught her attention. Grey's grip gave the impression this small dog was able to stop and start without warning. Pixie did do that from time to time. A solid grip on the leash kept her from running off. Follow the leader was underway.

A few feet from the car, Amie paused and waited until Pixie and Grey caught up with her. Grey switched the leash to his other hand. He held his hand out to her. Amie took a hold of Grey's hand and squeezed. Contentment. That was the one word the flashed through her mind. Grey hadn't answered her question yet. As they came to the end of the alley, she turned to him and asked, "Is it okay if I need to stay longer before I make up my mind about moving in?"

"My answer is simple. You can stay as long as you need or want. I hope you stay a long time. Mick's fun to have around. He isn't a great conversationalist." Grey grinned. "We can let Pixie and Mick keep each other company while we're doing the same. Sound like a plan?"

'Yeah. Why did you hesitate to answer when I asked the question before?" Amie pointed which way they needed to go.

Grey started down the walk letting Pixie lead. "Expectations, day dreams, and plans."

"Plans?"

"Pipe dreams. Stumbling blocks to open honest communication. To really hearing what you're saying. Not reading my interpretation into it. Make sense?" Grey stopped at the next corner waiting for the cross walk light to change.

"Some. It's about being present in the conversation and not figuring out what to say next too much." Amie started across the street with Pixie between her and Grey. There were pockets of clarity and ones of half-spoken words and pauses in their conversation. Maybe what they needed was a place where they could talk uninterrupted.

Grey nodded as they stepped up on the curb. "That's a lot of it. Some of it is about fear and uncertainty. What I'm about to say has nothing to do with you. It's me."

Amie paused as they reached the edge of the small park. Pixie began smelling the grass intently. "It'll take her a few moments to piddle. There's a trash can two benches over that has doggy waste bags and a can to dispose of them. We can walk over that way."

Grey held out the end of Pixie's leash to Amie. "Looks like the best smelling grass is on your side."

Amie took the leash. "Sure does."

They continued walking; stopping each time Pixie did until they reached the bench. Grey sat down and patted the section next to him. "Have a seat. I want to be sure you understand my answer."

Amie sat down next to him. "Okay. I think I get it. Go ahead."

Grey turned to Amie. "I want to be sure you know you're welcome to stay as long as you want."

"Thank you." Amie laid her hand on his and squeezed his. "I suspect we'll need to work things out."

Grey smiled. "Oh, probably. I'd like to suggest a base rule going in."

Amie leaned forward as Pixie pulled the leash taunt as she finished her business. "What is it?"

"We talk things out. Don't let things build up. Keep communication open and ongoing?" Grey stood. "I'll get the waste bag. You can give me your answer when I get back."

Amie tugged on Pixie's leash as Grey walked away. Pixie was ready to follow him. He'd won over the little scamp's heart within their first encounter. Much the same way he'd originally won her heart back when they first met fifteen years prior. They'd tried twice in that fifteen years to make a go of a relationship. Both times, they'd deepened their friendship and trust. Now were they going to try to recapture their past or had they moved on? She didn't know which one answered her gut reaction when Grey mentioned moving in with him. Maybe, just maybe, each of them had grown, changed and come full circle to a point where being together made sense and was a very real option.

Grey tore two bags off the roll of bags. He tilted his head back, looked up at the twilight filling sky. Edges of the setting sun streaked several of the clouds, adding pink and light golden streaks of color to them. The sky had looked much the same when he took Mick out for his morning walk. Hues and colors could add or detract from the moment, the mood, or emphasize a poignant thought. Somewhere in the course of their banter and conversation mix, they'd turned a corner, changed directions and were making headway, not moving backwards. Score a point for each of them, possibly many points, and a few high fives. He wasn't tallying anything until Amie made up her mind. As he turned around, he caught Amie watching him. Were her thoughts paralleling his? Was either of them ready to admit it? Be that honest with each other?

He walked back to where Pixie stood, gathered up her waste, and walked back to the trash can. He tossed the bag in the can and as he started to turn around, the clouds parted and a beam of sun light cut a narrow bright path across the grass between him and Amie. Talk about blatant signals. Grey glanced up, held up one hand, and gave the heavens a thumb up. He hadn't realized he been praying, but apparently the powers-that-be did.

Amie stood as he approached. She smiled, held out her hand, and moved closer. Pixie leaned against his leg as if she approved. What was Amie's translation?

# CHAPTER NINE

"Ready to go?" Grey asked as he took a hold of Amie's hand and entwined his fingers with hers.

"Sure am. I almost forgot I have an appointment with a supplier on Monday morning. I probably should drive my car to your place." Amie let go of his hand.

Grey swallowed twice, counted to ten forwards and backwards. He wasn't going to let his insecurity out. "I can bring you back Sunday afternoon or you can use my car. I'm working from home next week."

Amie faced him. "Grey, hear me out please."

He nodded. Shit, was she going to tell him she changed her mind?

"Unless your house is too small, which I doubt, I'm probably going to need more things. I like my independence and what if you need to go somewhere?"

"Two good points. Are you saying you're staying longer?" He stuffed both hands in his jacket pockets, swiping their sweatiness against the interior material.

Amie took a deep breath, held it, and let it go as she prepared her response. She didn't want to say she had made up her mind when part of her knew she needed to see the house, get the feel of the neighborhood and the commute, and know she and Grey were going to be able to set some ground rules going in. Their sexual attraction was still evident and a definite part of the equation. It was the small crap that neither she nor the guys she'd been involved with discussed that broke up her last couple of relationships. She wasn't going there again. Could she and Grey agree to create safe space and check in with each other about these things?

"I'm considering it. Remember I err on the side of caution with my decisions. Especially those that affect more than me. This is about you as well. Let's say I've learned to trust my gut and heart on important matters like this. I don't want either of us hurt."

Grey nodded. "Hearing you say that gives me peace of mind. I learned during my two years in therapy that trusting me included listening to me in the small quiet parts of the day and night. I so get where you're coming from."

Amie looked away, hoping she hadn't shown her shock when Grey said he'd been in therapy. She'd heard from a few of their mutual friends he'd stepped down from group social activities and dating about a year and half ago. The old Grey would have kept this secret. Another indication he'd changed. The pluses were adding up. Still part of her needed reassurance. To hear Grey say what he wanted without hiding. Damn, she needed to tell him too. When was the right time?

She raised her gaze until Grey's met hers. "I think we've got some things to talk about. Make sure we're on the same page and using the same definitions. No lost in translation."

Grey snorted. "For damn sure. That got us in more than one argument and tripped up more than a few people I know. One reason why I make doubly sure now my clients get what they and I agree to in black and white. Aka as my lawyer says legalese translated in layman's terms."

Amie grinned, and then added. "Oh, yeah. No need for a dictionary on a pedestal and two set of encyclopedias to dissect and debate what you're saying."

"Sounds like you and I have some things to talk about on the way to my place. You're still coming right?" Grey held out his hand.

Amie leaned down, picked Pixie up, and took Grey's hand. "Oh, yes I'm spending the weekend with you. I don't think we're going to have a problem talking. If we can get on to the important topics."

Grey stared at her for a few moments. He wet his lips as he held up two fingers. "It takes about forty minutes to get to my place. Do you mind making a list as we talk of the topics we agree we need to talk about?"

"Seriously, you want to make a list?" Amie kept pace with Grey as he started walking away from the bench.

"Yes I do. I want to be sure we focus on those topics. And get the more important ones at the top of the list." Grey pushed the crosswalk button. "Your thoughts?"

"I think the list is a place to start. I hope we don't get bogged down in what needs to be on the list and in what order." Amie set Pixie down after they crossed the street.

"Let's set our first ground rule, then. I say we need to each give five items that are important to us. We can build from there as needed." Grey paused at the corner of the alley.

Amie held up their joined hands. "I want our conversations to intertwine like our hands are."

Grey quickly brushed his lips across her cheek. He pointed at their hands. "Good symbol of how united we want to be. I'm willing to give it a shot."

"Me too. My first priority is food. You cooking or me?" Amie reached the car first.

Grey unlocked the car. Cooking. . .most Friday nights he ordered in or stopped by the market on the way home. Canned soup, grilled cheese, and a carton of eggs wasn't fancy eating. He could live on a bowl of cereal or microwaveable frozen dinners. He'd cut back on those since his doctor told him to cut back his salt consumption. He mentally inventoried the few items left in his fridge. Tomorrow he needed to get groceries and food for Mick. So tonight, who cooked wasn't as important as what got cooked. He turned toward Amie as he started the car. "We both are cooking. I got homemade pizza fixings. Unless you want to order in."

"Homemade pizza sounds good. Haven't had that in a while. Do you have microwave popcorn? A beer or two? Maybe some soda?" Amie fastened her seatbelt.

Grey laughed. "I'm not a big junk food person any more. I do have some popcorn and root beer. I think I might have a couple of pints of black cherry ice cream in the freezer too. Sound like a winning combination?"

"Sure does. We can mix the ice cream with the left over yogurt and sprinkles. There's a cozy mystery movie on tonight I've been trying to catch. Sounds like a good popcorn and root beer one." Amie smiled at him and settled back in her seat.

Grey knew that look, her look of intrigued excitement. Amie felt safe enough to go with him and take a chance on spending the weekend. Not the ending he pictured when he left his house four hours ago. His earlier thoughts had run along a pleasant lunch, reconnect with Amie, and ask her out. Now she was riding next to him, planning an evening's entertainment, talking about moving in, and bringing Pixie with her. A lot of changes from knowns to unknowns and to a blend of the two. Not what he could or would have envisioned given his tendency to rely on what he knew and experienced. It appeared fate and the powers that be were giving them a chance, a second chance to—to what he didn't know. His hopes, dreams, and yes aspirations leaned one direction. Could they sway in the breeze and bend like the willow? Flex as necessary? Frack, hesitating. Going with the flow made more sense than analyzing it. Besides, Amie had a pen in one hand and a small note pad in her other. Time to focus on the here and now.

She blew him a kiss and winked. Oh, yeah definitely time to focus on the here and now conversation. Fact was much better than any fantasy his mind could weave up for now.

Grey merged into traffic heading across town. Evening rush hour had thinned out some. Still bumper-to-bumper traffic would increase their trip to about fifty minutes. One-way streets added an extra ten miles to their drive. "What's your number one item for the list?"

# CHAPTER TEN

"Sex." Amie glanced at Grey as she wrote the word on the top line of the pad. Grey quickly glanced at her and back to traffic. Talk about gut level reaction. His mouth opened, closed, and opened again. He'd quickly snapped it shut and nodded. She pressed her lips together hoping to keep her mirth suppressed. Thoughts of shagging Grey had swamped her from the moment she saw him walk toward the table at lunch. Every year since they'd started meeting for lunch her hormones fixated on Grey and the chemistry they often ignored. It was like he oozed testosterone in a subtle way that reached out and caressed her libido rather discretely though her hormones claimed otherwise. The other thing about him that enveloped her was his natural smell. Grey wore little or no colognes. If he did, the scent was very minimal. His citrus and bergamot scent soap reminded her of a freshly brew cup of tea. Only once in their earlier relationship had she given in and nibbled his neck and ear. His reaction stayed with her as if it happened yesterday. There was no doubting his reaction. She wanted to dive deep into that passion again. Wait...make that over and over. She took a breath and paused her mental meandering. Grey deserved a response since he'd looked at her twice since they'd reached a stop light.

"It's not the only thing on my mind." She grinned as he looked at her and shrugged. "Though we've danced around our attraction and bantered about it often this afternoon."

"Yup. We have." Grey put the car in park and turned toward her. He pointed at the stop light. "My turn to add to the list for moment."

"Go ahead."

"Sleeping arrangements." Grey put the car in gear and returned to focusing on traffic.

Amie hastily added sleeping arrangements next to sex on the first line. "Good to see our priorities match."

Grey looked at her and blew a raspberry.

Amie chortled. "Ah, well. There are other things too."

"Glad you noticed." Grey put on the turn signal as he moved the car into the left turn lane.

Amie laid the pen and pad in her lap. "How much longer to your place?"

"About another twenty minutes?"

"My next topic might get settled by the time we get there."

Grey eased into the turn, watching pedestrians making their way across the intersection. He waited until he completed the turn to respond. "I'm listening."

"Well—er-er," Amie didn't say more.

"You at a loss for words? Come on. Get it out." He glanced at Amie. She wasn't looking at him. Lord, what could embarrass her more than talking about sex or sleeping arrangements?

He started to reach toward Amie when she spoke. "Not a word loss. Rather how to say it."

"Just say it. That's been a long time agreement between us."

"Yes. Still some subjects are touchier than others." Amie turned in her seat. "Like money. Division of labor. And independence."

Grey smiled. "Yeah. Good points. Here's my take. Before Mick, I had a cleaning service. Mick and I are bachelors. Soon to have housemates. I like easy to clean and care for."

"I think that needs a bit more explanation."

"Sure. I have hardwood floors, throw and area rugs, and a 'shoes off in house' policy. I keep a pair of slippers by the front and patio doors."

"Uhmm I think we may need to stop at the mall then."

"Why?"

"I didn't bring slippers."

Grey chuckled. "Not a problem. I can loan you a pair of slipper socks for tonight. Tomorrow we can see what the market has available when we grocery shop, okay?"

"No, Grey."

"No?" Grey asked as he slowed for another stop light.

"Yes, I said no. I want my own slippers. We passed the mall already. Where are we going to shop for them tonight?" Amie stared at him intently. The unsaid current vibrated between them ready to induce a possible argument. It wasn't worth the time or energy. The small shopping complex close to the house probably had what Amie wanted. He could pick up a few things as well. Items that he knew from their discussion at the shop he needed.

Grey took a breath, held it, and pictured his frustration leave him as he drove. Traffic had taken its toll. Trying to focus on their conversation, watch people j-walking, and drivers not paying attention had him on edge. Mick was in the doggy yard. He had his doghouse for shelter. Temperatures were dropping fast. A few snowflakes had come down as they drove. He exhaled and laid his hand on Amie's shoulder. "There's a small shopping complex two streets over from the house. The pharmacy there will have what you need. I've seen them there. I need to get a couple of things too. Do you need personal toiletries?"

"Thank you. I forgot them in my haste to pack. I can pick up travel size." Amie laid her hand on his.

"Since you're planning or thinking about staying longer or coming over more, why not get regular sized ones? I've got room on my bathroom counter or the hall bath for them."

"Was I that transparent? You read me? Or did you guess?"

Grey negotiated the turn into the shopping complex. He parked and faced Amie. "You talked about staying longer. That might include a week, a few days, or coming over more. I'm not reading anything into it. It's your decision to tell me."

Amie tapped the windshield and pointed. "Convenience Pharmacy and Market."

"That's the one." Grey pulled into a parking space close to the front of the store.

"I know this place. I shop the one on Burkett Ave near the hospital. Diane, the owner, talked about opening a second store. I left before she decided where." Amie opened her door. "Pixie, behave Momma and Grey will be back shortly."

Grey reached backed and patted Pixie as he unfastened his seatbelt. "Mind Momma. I'll bring you a treat if you're a good girl."

He got out and closed the door. Pixie let out a few yips and barks before lying down in the back seat again. Amie met him at the front of the car.

"Damn, it's gotten cold. The temperature has dropped." She pulled on her gloves.

"Sure has. Another reason I want to get home. I put Mick out in his play yard before I left for lunch. His doghouse isn't heated." Grey picked up his pace as he made his way to the pharmacy's entrance. "I've got a couple things to pick up. Meet me at the front of the store. We'll check out together."

Amie kept pace with Grey until they reached the entrance. "All right I need about ten minutes. You?"

"Sounds about right. Check in the food section before you go upfront. I may still be there." Grey walked away toward the back half of the store.

Amie checked out each aisle heading before going over two aisles and making her way midway down the aisle. "Socks, underwear, briefs, t-shirts and there they are. Slippers."

Backless slippers like her mother and grandmother wore. One size fitted small, medium, or large. She picked up the bright pink large sized ones and continued to the toiletries aisle. Toothpaste, toothbrush, and a small bottle of mouthwash joined the slippers in her basket. The last items she added were a bottle of her favorite shampoo and deodorant. She shook her head as she checked the items again ticking them off against the list on her phone. As she made her way back up the aisle, she stopped near the mark down shelves. The soft blue sweatshirt on the top shelf caught her eye. She checked the size. Extra-large, fluffy and the right price. She would stay warm in that if Grey kept the heat low like he had in their first apartment. She looked up, catching her expression in the mirror on the reading glasses rack. Unsure, frowning some and blurry eyed. Old memories kept popping up and uncertainty laughed at the back edge of her mind. Amie shrugged, turned, and made her way across the store toward the food area. She had better control than her subconscious thought, didn't she?

# CHAPTER ELEVEN

Amie sighted Grey as she neared the food section of the store. She turned down the aisle he occupied. He picked up one box off the shelf he stood in front of. Examined the box like he studied the wrapper and printing on it. He looked up, put the box back, and reached for another. He did the same with three others. Amie looked up noting the overhead aisle sign that read Feminine Hygiene and Sexual Health. Grey garnered more points for putting time and effort forth to be sure he got the right condoms. Her health mattered. Warmth surged through her. Grey was showing with his actions how much he cared and she mattered.

She knew that finding non-latex condoms wasn't easy. Amie faced Grey. "I've got what I need. You?"

He shrugged. "Not yet. I'm glad you're here."

"Oh?"

"All I'm finding are latex condoms. What brand do you use?" He pointed at the first two shelves. "All those are latex. I read the packages to be sure."

"I saw you did. Thank you." Amie moved closer to Grey, leaned in and kissed his cheek.

"You're uh-uh welcome." Grey quickly turned back to the shelves. Why did he feel like he got caught indecently exposed? He took a deep breath, exhaled and leaned down hoping it looked like he was trying to see the boxes on the shelf better instead of the flush he felt creeping across his cheeks and down his neck. "Can you tell me the name of the brand you use?"

Amie's soft chuckled didn't help. He swore his cheeks got redder along with his neck. Fifty-five years young and blushing like a teenager buying his first box of rubbers. It wasn't like he hadn't done this before. And with Amie too!

Amie walked behind him as she spoke. "The name brand box is blue and white. The comparable one is a silver and blue."

She squatted down next to him pointing at two boxes on the lowest shelf. "There's the labels for them. Damn, too far down for me to see if there are any further back."

Grey looked behind him, left, then right, and stepped back. "Move over and I'll take a look."

Amie looked up, squinting, her brows arched. "What?"

"Please move. I'll take a look." Grey leaned down until his hands touched the floor. He stretched his legs out behind him, going lower until he lay flat on the floor on his stomach. He turned his head sideways and reached into the open space between the shelves. "I think there's two boxes here. God, I hope they aren't expired."

"Me too. That's why I usually buy 2 boxes at a time." Amie stood as he pulled two boxes out and set them on the floor.

Grey rose on his hands and knees, looking up he scoffed. "Are you telling me you have supplies at home?"

"Do you think I'd do that to you?" Amie started to walk away.

"Wait," Grey said a bit louder than he wanted. He quickly got up and looked around. No one else was close by. He picked up the boxes after checking their expiration dates and trotted after Amie. "If you forgot them that's okay."

"I'm going to say this once. I don't want to talk about it until we're in the car, okay?"

Grey nodded. He knew that tone. Amie wasn't kidding. Her flat affect added the unsaid part. She didn't like being doubted. Man, had he stuck his foot in his mouth on that question.

"I didn't forget them. I've not needed condoms for quite some time. Now let's get what we need and go, please." Amie stared at him. Not looking away, but still a sense of sadness escaped her slamming straight into him, ramming itself deep into his heart. There was pain and yet a sense of trust too. She'd shared something that she hadn't before. Yes, he would honor her request and not discuss it more until she said she was ready to.

"We'll talk when you're ready. I've got a couple things to pick up for breakfast. Cinnamon rolls okay? Scrambled eggs and hash browns?" Grey pointed toward the cold case two aisles over. "I use their generic cinnamon rolls to and sprinkle extra cinnamon on them."

Amie nodded. "Homemade hash browns too?"

"Not this time. Toaster ones for now. What flavor coffee creamer you like in your morning tea or coffee?"

"Plain. Won't detract from the cinnamon and their iced sweetness." Amie stopped in front of the dairy section. "I eat yogurt too. A four pack will do. I've got the creamer."

Grey put a dozen eggs, two cans of cinnamon rolls, a bottle of cinnamon, and box of powder sugar in his basket next to the two boxes of condoms and two cans of dog food. He reached for Amie's hand as they walked up to check out area. Amie slight squeezed his and let go. She started to enter a separate checkout line. Grey hesitated, cleared his throat, and asked. "Do you mind if I pay for this?"

"I prefer to pay for my things." Amie placed her toiletries and slippers on the conveyor belt. "You can pay for the household items, all right?"

"That's fine." Grey got in line behind Amie. They'd figure out who paid for what if Amie moved in. He suspected she would if they both let their guard down. There was more at stake than good sex. That they had no problem with. Where their conversation went once they got in the car he wasn't sure. He did know as he waited for the cashier to ring up his purchase, Amie was still with him, spending the weekend with him, and had possible plans to stay longer. Those were positive steps and a goodness.

Grey put their purchases in the trunk, unlocked the door for Amie, and checked on Pixie who was asleep on the back seat. As he got in the car, he made a decision. One that caused his heart to speed up. It was the truth. One that he was willing to admit to himself. Not out loud yet. He hoped in the coming days he could.

Amie fastened her seatbelt. She ran her sweaty palms down her jeans, grateful Grey couldn't see her do it. She'd asserted herself and it felt good. Grey had created space for her to feel safe in doing that. Both their actions were emphasizing and supporting their words. Maybe her apprehension wasn't necessary. Could she calm her uneasiness and stay mindful that Grey wasn't her last two relationship attempts? Grey wasn't the same person he was when they broke up seven years ago. It was becoming more and more evident they'd both changed. Changed in ways that allowed them to be here. Here in a now that had the two of them working on moving in together again. Were they ready to admit it? Ready to say yes, let's be a couple again?

"I'm sorry I was curt in there. My last couple of relationships weren't great." She turned in her seat until she could see Grey easier. She caught his quick nod as he merged into traffic.

"I caught something was up. I'm ready to talk when you are." Grey laid his hand on hers and entwined his fingers with hers. "You tell me when you want to talk about it."

"I'd like to talk about it now." Amie started to pull her hand away. "That is if you're *ready*."

# CHAPTER TWELVE

"I'm ready if you are." Grey glanced in the rearview mirror. They had about ten minutes until they arrived at the house. Amie's tone plus emphasis on ready had him ready to roll his eyes. The unspoken poke about he best be ready or she wasn't sharing irked him. Yet, he didn't let go of his self-control. What Amie needed or had to say must be important for her. Otherwise why the tone and emphasis.

He waited until he stopped at the light at the next intersection to say more. "I want to hear what you've got to say. If you prefer to wait until you have my full attention, that's fine. We'll be at the house in about ten minutes."

Amie didn't pull her hand away. Her sigh practically echoed off the silence filling the car. Grey checked oncoming traffic and moved into the intersection. "I need both hands to complete this turn. Please tell me what's bothering you."

He inhaled, slowly exhaled, ready to change the topic when Amie spoke.

"I've not had sex in two years. Well couple sex. Wore out two vibrators. Last two relationships didn't even get to making out. One guy wanted someone to be a live-in maid. The other wanted a nanny for his grandkids while he and his daughter, and son-in-law globetrotted. Not great going if you know what I mean." Amie let go an exasperated sigh.

"Wha-t-t? Two guys thought you were only good for being hired help?" Grey turned right on the next street.

"Yes. My luck at picking guys has sucked sour—make that very sour lemons!" Amie pulled her hand out from under his.

"Honey," Grey grabbed Amie's hand. "There are some real dunderheads in the world. Those two make dickheads shine. You're worth more than that. Come on, you are special."

Amie sniffled. "Thanks. It's been a hard couple of years. Moving outside my nursing comfort zone. Work was my world, my main squeeze after my marriage blew up, even my almost second marriage. Dating became surreal thoughts after a while."

"You're not the only one who's made bad choices." Grey made two left turns and pulled into the driveway in front of him. "I had my last real date over a year ago. The lady I was interested in after I broke up with Sheila's mom kept saying she found me intriguing. Yeah right, we went out twice and she ditched me when her ex-husband came back to town. Talk about being played for a fool."

"Damn, Grey. It's like both of us have struck out unless it's you and me." Amie patted his arm. "Are we here?"

"Yes. Welcome to my place. Mi casa es su casa." Grey turned the ignition off and unfastened his seatbelt.

"Thank you. The house is lovely. The split foyer invites you in." Amie unfastened her seatbelt. "I do have one question before we go in."

"Sure. Ask." Grey opened his door. Pixie roused in the back seat.

"We made sure we have birth control. What about Pixie and Mick?"

Grey grinned. "Ah, ever practical. You don't have to worry. Mick is fixed. He's a terror at times when he gets rambunctious. I'm sure those two will chase each other for a bit. It's okay."

"Hard woods won't cause issues?" Amie got out and opened the back door, reached in and scooped up Pixie. "Don't want them running into things."

"Nah, the floors aren't polished. Mick has roughed some of them up already. Worst is when they bunch up a throw rug here and there." Grey unlocked the trunk and took their shopping bags out. 'Do you need help getting your tote and overnight bag out?"

"I can manage. May be I should take Pixie for a walk up and down the street for another poo and piddle break before we go in?" Amie set Pixie down and got her things out of the back seat.

"No need. She can use the doggy yard. Mick isn't territorial about his yard. Food yes. Yard no. I've found him and the neighbor's cat snoozing in his doghouse." Grey locked the car and started up the front steps until he got to the top step. He turned back near the top step. "Really it's okay. If you want to take Pixie out in the back yard close to the house there's a small patch of grass she can use as her potty area tonight."

"Thank you. I didn't bring her bed or crate. She usually sleeps with me." Amie started up the steps. Pixie followed her.

"I'm sure we'll figure something out. Most nights Mick is on the foot of my bed or in one of his beds." Grey unlocked the door. "Let's see what they do and go from there. Can't figure it all out ahead of time."

"You're right. I'm worrying to worry." Amie shrugged as Grey opened the front door. Gut flutters—damnable butterfly like twitters—lurched through her like a strong hurricane wind buffeting her forward. The path was clear. Nothing that unusual. Well except...she hadn't spent this much time with Grey in years. Their conversation centered around them. How they were going to accomplish. . .accomplish what? That part she still wasn't sure about. Why couldn't she go with the flow? When had having everything mapped out become so fracking important? Neither of them had control over what the other did or said. Damn, was she turning into a control freak?

"Hey," Grey said, laying his hand on her arm. "I've seen that look before. I give it to myself from time to time. It's fear talking. Fear loves to drive. It makes us do and say nutso things. When I voice mine, it takes the steam out of it and I'm back in control of me. Wanna share what's bothering you?"

"Inside maybe. Out here no. Too many ears." Amie walked up the steps, stopping when she got to open door. "After Pixie gets her last potty run, while we're cooking dinner, let's talk then."

"Sure. Go on in. We'll watch how Mick and Pixie interact with a fence between them." Grey stepped in to the house.

Amie watched Pixie jump up the short step into the house with her tail wagging, as she got closer to Grey. He'd won the little scamp over without much trying. A few pats and scratches along with a couple of treats from the bag he'd tossed in with his purchase as they made their way to the checkout added another hash mark in the plus column. Grey was racking up points by being himself. More and more she could see the pieces and glimpses she'd gotten of him from their interactions, talks, and short amounts of time together added up. Parts of his core that she admired and fell for as she got to know him the first time were still there. Shining brighter and beckoning all who got closer to go yes this is Grey. The other shining parts surrounding him like an aura. She could feel his energy—almost read it. Her psyche sighed and added its stamp of approval. Now if she could get her heart and gut to come to an agreement, maybe things would move forward in a clearer way. Were she and Grey going to get along? Would Pixie and Mick get along? Or was this another round of choosing sides and hoping for the best? Was she able to turn her doubt off and go with the flow?

Amie stepped into the house. She blinked twice. Glanced at Grey and moved further into the living room. The place reminded her of the apartment models she looked at. White walls, a few pictures here and there and plain colored furniture. It all went together. Yet it lacked...pizazz—personality and a feeling of home. Would Grey agree to change? Even small amounts?

"I like it to a point." Amie set her tote and overnight bag on the couch. It's medium brown tone called for a hint of color, like a multicolored throw. Some pillows. The patchwork-upholstered recliner in the corner near the front window could use an end table near it with a reading lamp. Was Grey still unpacking? He said he moved in a while ago.

Grey closed the door and locked it. He faced her with a puzzled look on his face. "You like it to a point?"

# CHAPTER THIRTEEN

Amie slipped her purse off her shoulder and faced Grey. "Yeah. It could use a woman's touch don't you think?"

"Depends on what you call a woman's touch. Some would want to totally redo the place. Paint, new furniture, adds things from their view. I like practical and esthetically pleasing." Grey started toward the kitchen. "Let me put these things away. Then we'll introduce Pixie and Mick."

"Sounds good. Need my help?" Amie and Pixie followed him.

"Sure. If you unbag things, I can put them away quicker." Grey set the bags on the eat-in counter. "Fridge stuff separate from other things, please."

Amie peered in the bag. "Eggs, half-n-half, cinnamon rolls, and yogurt out first."

Grey watched her put each next to the other on the counter close to him. He opened the fridge and reached for the eggs. "There's room for the yogurt on the middle shelf, okay? Or you like yours real cold?"

Amie came around the counter and stood next to him. "There's lots of room in there. You must eat out a lot or there's lots of stuff in the freezer."

"I do eat out when I work late. There are quick prep meals in the freezer. I learned to cook for more than one. Leftovers after two days lose their appeal."


60

"I know that feeling. I got a couple recipes I can show you that are easy and quick." Amie pointed to the middle shelf. "There is fine for the eggs and yogurt. Upper shelf for the half-n-half and rolls?"

"Yes." Grey took the items from Amie as she handed them to him. "Leave the other things. Pixie is sniffing near the patio door. Mick's barked a couple of times. Let's go and see how they take to each other."

"All right. Let me put her leash on just in case." Amie walked into the living room.

Grey combed his fingers through his hair as he pressed his lips together trying to suppress a yawn. They still had dinner to make and decisions to discuss. He glanced at his watch. It was six-thirty. Normally, he would stretch out on the couch and read or watch a movie. Lately he preferred working crossword puzzles or jigsaw puzzles while he listened to music. Working for himself had its perks and privileges. Being on the go a lot wasn't one of them. Deciding to keep his clients local or within a couple hours driving was panning out. Less travel time and those that wanted his consulting services outside that radius got it at a premium through online access or a set date for a meeting in person. His days of flying to three or four cities a week were done.

"Pixie, come," Amie called as she entered the kitchen. Grey watched Pixie sniff the bottom of the patio door again. The scamp turned toward Amie, wagged her tail, and turned back to the door. She started barking loudly. Amie called Pixie twice more. Pixie ignored Amie. Pixie barked and yipped more, refusing to move away from the door.

"I think Mick's got an admirer." Grey squatted down next to Pixie, holding his hand out to her. "Come on little one. Mama needs to put your leash on. Then we'll introduce you and Mick."

As if the brindle little scamp understood him, Pixie sat down next to him, her tail wagging rapidly. Grey looked up, motioned with his other hand for Amie to get closer. Amie rolled her eyes, nodded, and closed the space between them. She kneeled close to him, slipped two fingers under Pixie's collar, and snapped the leash into the hook. Pixie tilted her head back as if to say, "Mom was that necessary?"

"Okay, Pixie let's go meet Mick." Amie rose, grasping the leash in one hand.

Grey stood up, undid the lock, and slid the door open. Pixie tried to dart between him and Amie. "Pixie is in a rush. Yes, let's see where she heads first."

Amie stepped out on to the back patio. A rush of chilled air swept across her cheeks. Pixie shook, barked, and made a beeline toward the grass close to the end of the patio.

"Like most females I see." Amie laughed. "Got to make herself presentable before she meets her potential beau."

Grey chuckled. "Honey, you're beautiful just the way you are."

"Thank you, sir. I'll remind you of that when you see me first thing tomorrow morning." Amie unhooked Pixie's leash after she came back on to the patio.

Mick continued barking as Pixie approached the enclosed doggy yard. Amie took a hold of Grey's hand. "Can't tell if those are friendly barks or stay away ones."

"He's not growling. That's a good sign. Letting the two of them size each other up like this is good. Let's them check each other out." Grey moved closer to her.

Pixie walked up to the chain link fence wagging her tail as she yipped and barked. She squatted close to the fence and piddled. Mick lifted his leg and marked his area. Pixie moved to one side. Mick followed her. Their noses touched. Each backed up. More barks and yips sounded. Pixie got very close to the fence and sat down. Mick sniffed her, intently whined, and leaned against the fence, nuzzling Pixie as best he could.

"Truce or still sizing each other up?" Amie asked letting go of Grey's hand.

"Not sure. I'd say they're at peace with each other being around at the moment. They're going to get territorial some as they get used to each other." Grey slid his arm around her waist, hugged her, and let go. "Just like we're going to be doing too."

"Yeah. We've got separate rooms to retreat too. These two?" Amie shrugged.

Grey snorted. "If they get too growly, I'll get the two dog crates I have out."

"Best we open the gate and let our children decide friend or foe." Amie rubbed her hands together. "Out here or in the house?"

"Here first. Easier to corral them if they start fighting." Grey opened the gate and stepped back. Pixie didn't move. Mick ran to the edge of the open gate, hesitated, and ran back to where he'd nuzzled Pixie through the fence. He nuzzled her twice, turned, and ran out the open gate. He ran up to Grey, stood on his hind legs, pawing Grey's pants until Grey petted him. Mick dropped on all fours, turned like his tail was on fire, and bolted toward Pixie.

Amie rubbed her lips together, glanced at Grey, ready to say something when Grey held his hand up. He closed the space between them. "We're ready if necessary."

Amie nodded, her gaze on the couple sniffing and wagging their tails in front of them.

Pixie stood up, touched her nose to Mick's, and backed up. Mick sat down, yipped, and looked at Grey and Amie. Grey burst out laughing. "Mick, I can't explain women any better. We learn as we go my friend. Welcome to the party."

Amie cuffed Grey on the shoulder. "You telling truth or fibbing?"

"Shhh, Mick will hear you. I can't BS him. He understands me too well. Like Pixie gets you." Grey turned, holding his hand out to Amie. "How about pizza making?"

"I think we need to feed these two love birds first. That is if we can get them into the house." Amie pointed at Mick and Pixie. The two were enthralled with checking each other's scents out.

"Oh that is pretty easy with Mick. Watch." Grey walked to the patio door, rapped on it and called out. "Mick! Dinner! Eats!"

Mick backed away from Pixie like she farted, turned, and bolted for the patio door. Pixie stood up, yipped, and dashed off following Mick. Amie winked at Grey, walked up to him, kissed his cheek, and said, "Lead the way sir. Let the pizza making and feeding the kids commence."

Grey waited for Amie to enter the house first. He wondered if she realized how far they'd come since lunch. She was here for the weekend. They had their first difference of opinions. They were still bantering back and forth. Things were progressing. How much they were in agreement he didn't know. Would their frankness continue as they got closer to bedtime? Desire, need, and want didn't always play nice or together very well. Were they going to this time?

# CHAPTER FOURTEEN

*Three hours later*

Grey settled back against the couch. Dinner prep had gone well. Amie had shown him how to take the canned pizza dough and roll it out to make two thin crust pizzas. They had leftovers for lunch tomorrow. As soon as she finished the dishes, he'd broach the subject that kept using large elephant sized holding queues in their to be discussed list. One thing Amie had alluded to during dinner was her need for space. That part he could fulfill. Four bedrooms, a large dining area, and the family room that he used as his office along with the combination den and library were available depending on her need. Was she thinking housemate or lover? That topic really needed a decision.

"Okay, the dishes are done. Pixie and Mick are finishing their treats. Do you want to watch TV or listen to music?" Amie sat down on the opposite end of the couch.

"Neither. I'd like to talk about a couple of topics that came up this afternoon and evening." Grey kicked off his shoes and put his feet up on the coffee table.

Amie took off her slippers and put her feet up on the couch. "Do you mean sex and my moving in?"

Grey rocked back. She'd laid it out. He hadn't expected that. So she noticed the elephant patches on the discussion list. "Right to the point. Okay, let me phrase my main question this way, how much space are you needing?"

Amie hugged her knees to her. "Personal space some. Private space some. Shared space probably there will be a lot. Why?"

"I work from home often. I need quiet for conference calls. With two dogs, there's going to be time when they're barking and being rowdy."

"Good point. I don't work from home. I do bring bookkeeping home from time to time. Easier to do without customers and employees around. I use my laptop. I have a corner desk I can put in the den you showed me earlier."

"Are you saying you're moving in?" Grey scooted to the end of the cushion he sat on.

Amie refused to look at him for several moments. "Well," she began, "I'm seriously considering it. Your master suite is the size of my current place. Add in the room to let Pixie romp with Mick. Your companionship and shared space is an offer that would be hard to turn down flat."

Grey rose, moved sideways in the space between the coffee table and couch until he was inches from Amie. He sat down and turned so he faced her. "I don't think those two hellions would be very happy if we separated them either." He pointed to where Pixie and Mick lay curled up against each other on the throw rug they'd took turns messing up and playing tug of war with after they ate.

Amie laughed. "No, if Mick can howl as bad as Pixie can when she is upset—shrill doesn't begin to describe it."

Grey chortled. "Oh, Mick can howl. Off key is on key for him. One of the neighbors' kids has a garage band and sometimes the high pitch notes get Mick to singing along."

"So we may get serenaded some evening. Okay. Note to self. Get some ear plugs next time I am at the pharmacy." Amie grinned and swung her legs down off the couch. She scooted closer to Grey. "Now as to sleeping arrangements. . ."

Grey looked at her, arched an eyebrow, and winked. "Are you making a pass at me?"

"Nah. I've already made several of them at you. You've done it to me too." Amie slipped an arm around Grey's waist and hugged him. "My answers to mine are yes. How about yours?"

Grey ducked his head, his shoulders shaking. Snickers and snorts sounded. He looked up at her, his lips pressed together like he tried to keep from smiling or laughing. He pointed at her, shook his finger, and...fell out laughing. Grey wiped his eyes twice. "Oh, that is a grand come back and response! You caught me off guard good with that one!"

Amie licked one finger and drew a line vertically in the air. "Somehow yelling score just isn't quite right."

Grey put his hand over his mouth. His shoulders shook harder. Several moments passed as they shared their mirth. Grey used the hem of his t-shirt to wipe his eyes. "I think we've sufficiently broken the ice. Dare I put your bag in my room?"

"Oh, yeah. Make sure you put the condoms in there too. We might need them before the night is over." Amie kissed Grey's cheek. "Before that how about some cuddling?"

Grey inhaled slowly, lowered his hand, and glanced at her. He wasn't an easy face to read. Grey's poker face got him through a lot of shit. Some she'd witnessed firsthand. Tonight, he wasn't hiding his reaction. Man, could he blush or as quite a few guys put it have their face flush.

Grey leaned forward, resting his elbows on his knees. "You know there was a time when we would have hinted at this or spent moments trying to translate what wasn't said."

"Sure was." Amie didn't look away.

"Now we don't need twenty questions, guesswork or even too many probing questions." Grey started to rise. "I think our chaperones need one more potty run before we head for the bed."

"I agree. Think we need to crate them? You know keep them from popping on to the bed and interrupting things?"

Grey stood upright and stretched. "Probably wouldn't hurt. Two cold noses running across legs or arms are mood breakers for sure."

Amie laughed. "Much less the two of them setting on the edge of the bed staring at us while we get amorous."

"Might be a good idea to put them in together. With that rug their on too. Maybe a couple of treats too." Grey walked to where Amie's tote and overnight bag sat on the floor close to the hall entrance leading to the other half of the house. "I'll get the crate set up. Mick will go out when you open the patio door."

"Okay, meet you back here in say five minutes?"

. "Sounds good." Grey called out as he started down the hall.

Amie slide her feet into her slippers. She walked over to where Mick and Pixie lay sleeping on their sides. The pair looked like they'd done this for years. Neither was too far from the other. Amie scooped Pixie up and kissed the top of her head as Pixie started to rouse. Mick raised his head, his tail wagging. He jumped up, stretched, and started following her. "Come on Mick. Potty time. You too Pixie."

Amie set Pixie down close to the patio door. Mick nuzzled Pixie and moved closer to the door. Amie opened the door some. Mick shot out the door with Pixie following him. Snowflakes blew in through the open door, dancing above the tile floor for a few moments before landing on the floor and melting. A blast of wind pelted the door, rattling it as it tried to reach further inside while wrapping its icy fingers around whatever was in its reach.

"Winter hasn't given up yet." Grey walked up behind her.

Amie glanced over her shoulder. "Doubt it will for a few more weeks. Dang groundhog let his astonishment at seeing the sun overwhelm him too much."

Grey's warm breath caressed her neck as he slid his arms around her waist. "See the sun and a shadow, six more weeks of cold and snow. No shadow or sun supposed to herald spring is here. I don't know about you. Either way to me is a good enough reason to snuggle and pleasure a person you care about and enjoy being with."

Amie swallowed hard. Grey had tapped into her feelings like he read her mind. Somewhere in the last three hours, she'd slipped further away from the idea of friends with benefits and deeper into passionate caring coming closer to the L word. She inhaled sharply as Grey cupped her breasts. His lips floated across her neck sending images of butterflies fluttering from flower to flower-sipping nectar. Her eyes started to close. . .

Mick darted between their legs with Pixie following close behind him. To finish off the mood busting moment, a large blast of iced air swirled around them and back out the door. Great, how were they going to get back in the mood?

# CHAPTER FIFTEEN

"Talk about a mood killer." Amie patted Grey's cheek and started to move away. "Man it's gotten cold out there."

Grey took her hand. "It has. No mood dampener here. Just more determined to find that crate and get our two hellions corralled."

"You sure?" Amie hastily shut the patio door and locked it.

"Going to take more than a cold wind and two rambunctious pups to do that." Grey brushed his lips over hers. "I'm going to get that crate out of the closet. You find the two mini whirlwinds, ok?"

What could she say? Yes? No, you do it? She ducked her head, pressed her lips together, hoping her mirth didn't leak out. Her quirky sense of humor got ignited somewhere and it wasn't settling down. Anyone who thought Pixie and Mick were mini whirlwinds underestimated them. The blur that shot in through the door and between their legs moved like the wind that followed them in had goosed their backsides good. Amie inhaled and exhaled twice before she looked up. "Oh, yeah I'll find them just have the crate ready to corner them."

Grey smiled as he turned. "That's the easy part. Mick loves the gas fireplace in my bedroom. I turn it on and put his fave heavy blanket in the crate along with the rug he's shared with Pixie and—Viola, in the crate he goes and curls up."

"Sounds great. Pixie may fuss a bit. I'll bring some newspaper back to put in there too. She may need to piddle before we wake up." Amie picked up the paper off the coffee table.

"I've got puppy pads we can use too. When Mick travels with me, they come in handy." Grey pointed toward the TV as he started down the hall. "Looks like our culprits have settled in."

Amie glanced to where Grey had pointed. Pixie and Mick each sat on part of the throw rug they'd slept on earlier. Their tails started wagging faster as she approached. Amie shook her head. There was no mistaking the welcome she and Pixie had received. Warm, inviting and embracing. They were part of the in crowd of the occupants of this house and home.

"Bedtime, Pixie." Amie petted Mick before she picked Pixie up. Mick stood and followed her toward the bedroom. Grey met them at the bedroom door.

"Fireplace switch is on the left wall closest to the bathroom. Turn it on, please. I'll be back with their throw rug in a moment." Grey exited the bedroom.

Amie walked over to the crate. There was enough room for Pixie and Mick to curl up separately or together. Mick went up to the crate sniffed it and back to the bed where he rose on his hind legs. Resting his front paws on the bed, he stretched toward Pixie who lay close to the edge of the mattress. Amie smiled watching the pair. Their tails wagged faster each time their noses touched. Some might call it an instant love connection. She wasn't sure how to describe it except to say there was a definite connection and friendship between Mick and Pixie.

That was how she and Grey first put their attraction into words. They'd worked hard to get past their mutual and individual pain points after they realized how strong their friendship remained even after their breakup.

Amie turned on the fireplace and turned until her back was to the wall, allowing her to see Grey's room from a very distinct perspective.

She'd noted the king-size bed, the rich dark, and lightwoods along with the deep teal blues and burgundy accents when she first entered the room. Now her panoramic view sharpened her insight into Grey's tastes in decorating.

The patchwork quilt on the bed highlighted the center of the room, the king-size bed. A chester drawer set and a medium dresser lined the wall common with the living room. She noticed how quiet the neighborhood was earlier as they introduced Pixie and Mick. Grey had set up the room to take advantage of the sound buffering furniture placement offered. The white walls stood out even with the array of color with the quilt, wood tones from the dressers, bed frame, and headboard. The walls needed color. Color that gave the room warmth and invited its inhabitants in. Lord, she sounded like Charlotte and Roberta as they discussed afghan and quilt patterns with customers. Colors, choice, who was the craft for and its use. Amie rolled her eyes, snickered at her thoughts of how she could help Grey make his place over.

"What's so funny?" Grey asked, entering the bedroom. He'd stood out in the hall watching Amie for a few moments. He liked what he saw. Her in his room—soon to be their room? He didn't know. Well his heart and conscience knew what he wanted. Amie here with him and more than just a housemate. He wasn't sure when his feelings started changing, or moved deeper and closer to the heart portion of the L word. Things had and he wasn't arguing with himself over it any longer. They deserved another chance, more than a second chance. Could they make the step into loving each other again?

"My interior decorator alter ego. I'm off work and my mind is still color- coordinating things and envisioning projects." Amie shook her head. "Some nights it's hard to leave work at work."

Grey chuckled. "Well you haven't been able to leave work at work. Home and work have been the same place for a bit."

"Oh so true. Another reason why I'm looking for a place." Amie laid open sheets of newspaper on the bed. "I think these two are ready for more cuddling."

As if on cue, Pixie jumped down off the bed and walked over to where Mick lay on the floor near the fireplace. She sniffed the air with her nose, nuzzled Mick, and lay down beside him. She rested her head on his back near his front legs.

"Appears so." Grey closed the space between him and Amie. He leaned in, put his hand on her shoulder, and nibbled her neck.

"You taking hints from Mick?" Amie smiled, reached up, and patted his hand.

"Could be. How about you?" Grey moved past Amie. "Taking hints from Pixie?"

"Hmmm. Maybe." Amie folded all the sheets of newspaper together and picked them up. "Warmth. Comfy bed. Someone I like....hey cuddles are so much better when you do them with someone you like."

Grey snickered. "Good reply! Well let's get these two settled and I'll show you how much I like you."

Amie laid the newspapers on top of the crate. "Ooh. Did you just make a pass at me?"

"Could be. Now let's get our two lovebirds inside. Then I'll show you what I'm talking about." Grey smoothed the throw rug out on one side of the crate. He arranged the puppy pads next to it and placed the newspaper on top of them.

"Come on Mick. Bedtime. Pixie, you too." Grey patted the top of the crate. Mick rose, stretched, and entered the crate.

Pixie hesitated close to Amie. "Go on, sweetie. Mama is right here. Sleep tight."

Grey reached into his pocket and pulled out two dog biscuits. He held one out to Mick. "Here ya go, boy. Bed time treat."

He held out the other one toward Pixie. "You want a treat too?"

Pixie entered the crate, her tail wagging. She sat down near Mick and looked up at Grey. Grey placed the biscuits by each of them and latched the crate door. Munching and crunching followed.

Grey turned, held out his hand to Amie, and said, "Oh, yeah I made a pass at you. I'm ready to follow up with a warm shower together and some passionate cuddling in bed."

Amie sat down on the bed. She combed her fingers through her hair. Her gaze didn't meet his. What was going on? Had things changed and he missed read the nonverbal communication? Talk about ...

Amie looked up, grinning. "I'd forgotten how delicious showering together can be. You've got a good idea. But—how long has it been since we've seen each other naked?"

Grey snickered and snorted. "A few years I suspect. We've never had trouble with shucking our clothes around each other. It's been a while since we were lovers. Are you feeling uneasy about leaving the lights on?"

# CHAPTER SIXTEEN

Amie rose and walked over to Grey, not stopping until they stood toe-to-toe. "Lights don't bother me. I've seen me naked plenty of times. You've seen you too. Is this all about sex? Or is there passion, desire, and caring mixed in?"

She unbuttoned the cuffs of her blouse as well as the bottom button on her blouse. "Well?"

Grey leaned forward, clasped her hand, and whispered. "I gave up wham, bam, thank you ma'am in college. There's passion, darling, Lots of caring and desire, too."

"Good. Then how about some slow and steamy hugging and kissing?" Amie undid a few more of her blouse buttons. "You know the kind that tends to fog up your glasses and make taking your clothes off worthwhile?'

Grey reached down grasp the hem of his shirt and started pulling it up. "I'm in. I've always liked slowly undressing each other as we hug and kiss. Its sexy and a turn on to do this together at a pace that strokes both our passions hotter with each touch, caress and kiss."

Amie stopped unbuttoning her blouse. She moved as tight to Grey as she could. With her arms stretched out to her sides, she spoke. "Then what's holding you back?"

Grey rocked back some. He blinked, looked away, and right back at Amie. Her gaze met his straight on. A small grin curled her lips. Her determined look told him all he needed. She'd issued the challenge. Was he answering the call or backing down? Damn,

Amie was reading him good. He swallowed, flexed his hands, and reached for Amie. He'd been busy planning his tactful approach without considering Amie's needs or desires. Communication, the vital part of getting this to move forward and doing it *now*.

"Thinking instead of doing." Grey tugged his shirt off, tossed it on the bed, and slipped both arms around Amie. He tilted his head, lips puckered as he leaned closer.

Amie lowered her arms and laid her hands on his shoulders. Her gaze never left his. The closer he got, the more she smiled. She winked, puckered her lips, and got even closer to him. Grey took one last look, noting Amie's lips still slightly curled at the tips. He closed his eyes as he brushed his lips against Amie's. She didn't pull away. Her lips parted as she tangled her fingers in his hair.

Soft and light. Just the way she remembered the last time she'd touched him like this. Tightly hugging each other as they acknowledged their mutual desire. Seven years ago. That night had turned into a twelve-hour period of nude cuddles and naps in between discussions about what they each wanted from their friendship. Friends with benefits had happened now and then. They'd been through a lot during their tenure as friends, lovers, and even their three years as a couple. What was different this time was—her heart skipped a beat and her psyche whispered the L word. Maybe her heart and psyche were on to something. Now wasn't for deep thinking and analysis. It was time to reconnect with their mutual passion and express their feelings with actions instead of words and wariness. That was her plan. Though going with the flow made more sense. Be in the moment.

She eased the tip of her tongue through her parted lips as Grey deepened the kiss. His lips parted and their tongues met. Each sipped and tasted the other, renewing their chemistry and physical touch. Grey tasted of pepperoni, pizza sauce and the sharp romano cheese they added to the mozzarella slices on top of the Italian seasoned dough. Hints of the wine they'd drank welcomed her as she followed him into his mouth. Each breath she took sent whiffs of his aftershave mixed masculine scent toward her. Grey's tongue met hers. Tasting and dueling continued until Grey pulled back.

"We're too dressed." Grey unbuttoned the top two buttons of her blouse. He cupped her face. "Do we undress ourselves or help each other?"

Amie unclenched her hands, letting go of the strands of Grey's hair she held. She inhaled and exhaled slowly. Helping each other undress sounded a bit titillating...undress themselves would get it done faster and easier. She pressed her lips together as an image flashed through her mind. Oh, yeah! Hot and sexy that would awesomely be. She licked her lips, ready to answer Grey.

"How about we each take a piece of clothing off one at a time watching each other?" Amie undid two more buttons leaving only two more to undo.

Grey nodded. "Okay, I'll go first." He undid his belt, unbuttoned, and unzipped his jeans. He shoved them part way down his hips. "Shall I go further?"

Amie shrugged. "You went first when you took off your shirt."

Grey grinned and took a hold of her blouse. "Then how about you even things up and take this off?"

Amie looked away, up and down not meeting Grey's gaze for a few moments. "You know," she began, undoing one button. "I've imagined this from time to time. Fantasized about it, too."

"Oh honey, I've done the same. Our love making never lacks." Grey sat down on the bed. "It's our timing that sucked."

"I think we needed to grow, find ourselves, and understand what we have." Amie undid the last button, slipped the blouse off her shoulders and down her arms.

"Probably. I know I'd be interested and you were in another relationship."

"Or you moved away or were seeing someone." Amie tossed her blouse on top of Grey's t-shirt.

"We got it right this time." Grey stood, motioning for her to turn around.

"Why?" Amie asked, turning around.

"I want you nude. You want me nude." Grey unhooked her bra. "Time to help each other get out of these clothes."

Amie glanced back at Grey. He smiled, kissed her shoulder and added, "Seeing you naked is a hot turn on for me."

"Grey, you said naked. Not nude." Amie tried to turn around.

"Stand still." Grey pulled her bra straps off her shoulders and down her arms. "Yeah, I did. Naked is so hot and gets me hotter."

As Grey began exposing her breasts, she covered his hands with hers. "Sorry I need some reassurance. You're sure about this?"

Grey pulled his hands out from under hers, took her hand, and slowly turned her around until she faced him.

"Yes, I am damn sure. And this should back me up." He lowered their hands until they were level with his crotch. He flexed his hips forward. His hard cock rubbed back and forth against her fingers.

On his next thrust, she partially closed her fingers around him and gently squeezed. Grey groaned. "Oh sweetie, enough. I'm on the edge right now."

"So am I. Touching you like this is exciting. I'm getting very wet." Amie let go of her bra. "I think we need to get out of these clothes now and into the shower."

Grey nodded, lowering his hands. Her bra fell down. Grey looked down and back up, smiled and shoved his briefs and jeans over his hips and cock. A metal plink sounded as his belt buckle and jeans hit the floor. Next were his socks. Heat rolled off Amie's twice over gaze up and down him.

Soon Amie's clothes joined his in a pile on the floor and bed. Her flush told him all he needed to know. His gaze up and down her heated her up like hers had him. Grey kicked their pile of clothes aside and held out his hand. "I want to run my soapy hands and lukewarm water all over you."

"*Great!* I got the same need." Amie took his hand, raised it to her lips, and suckled each of his fingers. "Let's get you clean. I need to taste you."

"Oh, darling. The need is mutual." Grey leaned down and swept Amie up in his arms. "I call dibs on washing you."

# CHAPTER SEVENTEEN

"Grey, I'm too heavy. Put me down." Amie looped her arms around his neck.

"Not that heavy." Grey helped Amie stand up close to the walk in shower. "I don't have the stamina I used to."

Grey opened the cabinet close to the dual shower. He laid two marine blue bath sheets on the counter. He opened the door to the enclosed dual head shower.

"You still have a nice butt." Amie patted his arse cheeks as he leaned in to turn on the shower.

"Thank you. I still enjoy looking at you as we are now. Nude, here with me, touching me and eager to make love." Grey leaned back, brushed his lips over Amie's and stepped into the shower. "Lukewarm water and soap. A delicious way to get my hands all over you."

Grey ducked his head under the shower, picked up a bar of soap and began working up lather with it. Amie entered the shower behind him, pulling the door closed behind her. "Dual heads. Makes showering together nice."

"Not if you're at the opposite end of the shower. Close together makes things much nicer. Don't you think?" Grey laid the soap in the soap dish and reached for Amie.

"I like soap *and* water. Not just soap. Makes washing each other much more fun." Amie stuck her hand in the water. "Move over. Share the water. Or I turn on the other showerhead."

Grey stepped out of the spray of water, held out his soapy hands, and grinned. "Can I help you get wet and soapy?"

Amie tittered. "I don't know. You seem to be eager to douse all of me. I might not want a wet head." She moved into the shower spray tipping her head back.

"I've got a blow dryer. I don't plan on going to bed with a wet head either. We don't need colds." Grey put his soapy hands on her shoulders, massaged lightly, and slid them part way down her back.

Amie soaped her hands, glanced at Grey, and issued her challenge. "Move back so we soap down each other or..." She didn't say more.

Grey opened his mouth, closed it, looked away, and stepped back. "I want to touch you. No, make that I need to touch you. I want you bad. Quickies just don't ..."

"Yeah, it's like a lit match that flares and fizzles at the same time." Amie placed the soap bar in the niche and faced Grey.

Grey looked down at his soapy hands and back up at her. He grinned and stepped closer. "Preference where I start?"

Amie laughed. "You got my shoulders already. I think it's my turn to decide where I start."

"I'm all yours." Grey put his hands up over his head. "Well at least where you want to start soaping."

Amie rubbed her hands together, slicking her palms with more soapsuds. She reached out, cupped Grey's balls, palmed them slightly, and stroked up and down his cock. Slow, faster, then slow again. Grey groaned, lowered his arms until his hands rested on her breasts.

She let go of Grey's cock, pressed her palms against his groin and stroked up wards. Some women adored a six-pack set of abs. Guys who worked out were eye candy for sure. Too many of the ones she'd met or dated were too focused on their idea of fit and toned. Grey took care of himself. Worked out some without obsessing on his measurements. He'd told her more than once he liked her full curves and self-confidence. That turned him on he said at the height of passion a couple of times. Here they were now and Grey was showing her with his actions and words how integral this was.

Sliding her hands upwards, she closed the space between them. Grey cupped her breasts, rubbed his thumb pads over, around and back across her nipples until they were almost as hard as his cock.

Amie swept her hands in broad circles up and over Grey's stomach until she reached his hips. A quick swipe across the part of each ass cheek she could reach brought her even closer to Grey. He leaned down, his lips parted as his lips touched hers. Her lips parted wanted—no needing to taste Grey again. There was an overwhelming need to capture his essence and embed within her memories and taste buds. Deep within her psyche, a small voice whispered what if this doesn't work out. It might not. She wasn't letting fear drive or grab her focus. Here and now, she and Grey were in agreement. They desired each other and mutual pleasure was their intent.

Her tongue met his. Dueling like before, chasing, and tagging each other as they sipped and savored each other's subtle tastes and essences.

Grey copied her strokes up and down, over and round as soap slicked their bodies. His hands moved lower, across her mons until he touched her clitoris.

"Yes," Amie said, breaking off their kiss. "My nipples and clit are so sensitive."

Grey put his arm around Amie's waist, pulling her tighter to him. "Relax. Let it happen. I've always loved pleasuring you. A small orgasm before we rinse, please?"

Amie nodded, nestling closer to him. Grey knew the time for talk and words was past. He snuggled Amie against him as he increased pressure and speed with each stroke across her taut clit.

With his other hand, he captured her nipple between the pads of his thumb and forefinger, pulling and twisting it in a counter rhythm to each stroke of her clit.

Amie's soft sighs of pleasure grew more intense with each stroke and tweak. Her gaze met his. The flush he loved to watch that told of her rise and ride to the crest of her orgasm started just above the v of her cleavage and spread upward. One shudder, then another rippled through her and on to his fingers showing and telling him she was very close.

"Oh, my" Amie moaned. "So close. *So clooose.*'

Amie's eye closed. She moaned and shuddered twice more. Grey slowed his strokes, let go of Amie's nipple and held her close until her clit stopped spasming.

Amie inhaled and exhaled twice, wet her lips and opened her eyes. Grey's smile and gaze greeted her. He brushed his lips softly over hers. She inhaled again and let go a deep sigh. "Wow."

Grey laid his finger on her lips. "I agree. Let's rinse before we run out of hot water."

She nodded, stepping under the spray and rinsed. She kissed Grey's cheek, and exited the shower. Grey rinsed, turned the shower off, and accepted the towel she held out. Taking turns drying each other off in between more kisses and caresses, she noticed her and Grey's smiles in the mirror. Somewhere in their short time in the shower, they'd bonded in a new way. A place of knowing and shared pleasure. Her voice of doubt had quieted. Her psyche and heart knew she was where she belonged at this moment in time.

Grey yawned twice as he hung up the towels. Amie pointed her finger at him, ready to shake it and tell him stop yawning. "Grey," she said—no more words came out as a huge yawn overcame her.

"Yeah, we're both ready for sleep." Grey looked down. "Not all of me is ready to sleep."

Amie cupped Grey's testicles, squeezed them slightly, and let go. "I'm not quite ready to sleep either. First one in bed gets to call the position."

Amie quickly exited the bathroom.

Grey chuckled as he followed. He'd already decided to let Amie chose their loving making position. "I'm game. Just remember there's no chandelier in there."

"Damn, that takes my first choice out of the running." Amie swept the covers back and rolled on to the bed.

"Can you imagine explaining repair needs to the contractor patching the ceiling?" Grey sat on the edge of the bed. "Remember Rachel and Terry?'

Amie burst out laughing. "*Oh, do I.* The look on the contractor's face as he walked out after giving them an estimate for their kinky playroom and the need for reinforced hooks from the ceiling for their swing. The man never came back."

"Yup. Took Terry awhile to find a contractor within the leather community to do the work for them. I'm glad we never took them up on their offer to try things out." Grey opened the nightstand drawer. He took out the box of condoms. He turned and faced Amie. "How about we get wild and wooly under the covers?"

"Oh, yes. I'm ready for some more hot touches and cuddles." Amie rolled on her side, facing him. "I'll tell you my second fave position after I taste you."

Grey propped up his pillows and lay back on the bed. "All right. I get to taste you too."

# CHAPTER EIGHTEEN

"One at a time? Or our fave number from the Chinese takeout place around the corner from our first apartment?" Amie grinned and winked at him twice.

"Number sixty-nine was easy then. Ten years younger and much more flexible. Let's try that another time." Grey lay back against the pillows, holding his hand out to Amie.

Amie scooted closer to Grey. "Certainly. Hand me a condom, please."

Grey opened the box, took out a foil wrapper, and offered it to her palm up. "You want me to unwrap it?"

"Open it. I'll get it in a moment." Amie got on her knees. She wet her fingers, gently wrapped them around Grey's cock, and kissed his cockhead.

"Honey, don't tease. I'm in between ejaculating and falling asleep. Once is all I've got tonight." Grey eased his fingers between her legs, inserting a finger into her.

"I'm close too. Let me taste you without distraction." Amie opened her lips, taking Grey into her mouth. Over and across, again and again she licked, savoring Grey's saltiness until his thrusting into her mouth increased. She encircled him with one hand, drew her cheeks inward—tightening her suction on him and slowly withdrew him from her mouth.

"Oh, that's good." Grey touched her arm. "Much more and I'm going to come."

Amie nodded as she let go of Grey and turned partway toward him. "Time for the condom."

"Shortly. Let me get a taste of you. Lay back and let me check how wet you are." Grey patted the bed.

Amie rolled on to her side and lay next to him. She parted her legs as she laid her hand on his. "I'm ready."

Sultry and husky. . .Amie's whispered readiness focused his attention—make that grabbed him deep down in his groin, tightening his balls tighter to him. Another time, he'd be between her legs, her clit exposed, ready for one kiss after another from him. Tonight . . .tonight was for reconnection, cuddling and finding release before they slept. Part of his psyche cheered his caring while his male hormones, drunken ego, and Id hissed and booed. He shoved the drunk louts away with a promise that he'd kiss Amie's clit properly at another time.

He laid his hand on Amie's stomach, stroked downward until her pubic hair caressed his fingers. Soft. . .like the down of a kitten's fur, the hair on top of a baby's head, and soft as the feathers he found on the ground outside the cabin on their first get away weekend together. Some things didn't change. Some did. Like the place Amie held in his heart and psyche. Pleasuring her was as important as his own release. Yet, sleep called, demanding its lure and priority took precedence over everything else. Not yet, his male hormones yelped sending another jolt of energy and focus forth.

Grey stroked lower until the pad of his finger slipped over Amie's clitoris. Swollen, taut, and dewy with her wetness. Around and over like she had with him. He caressed lower, lubing his finger more. Up and over, back and forth. Each stroke told of how turned on Amie was. She moved and rubbed against him, moaning softly.

"Much more and I am going to come again." Amie grasped his wrist. "I need you inside me."

Grey nodded, leaned over, and brushed his lips across hers. He pulled back, raised his hand, and stuck the tip of his tongue out. One lick, two licks as he worked his finger in and out of his mouth.

On the third lick, he withdrew his finger. "Wonderful. Sweet and salty just as I remember."

Amie smiled, holding up the condom. "Time for this?"

Grey lowered his arm. "Oh yeah. Definitely time."

Amie rolled on her side, cupped Grey's testicles, their warmth and firmness rested against her palm. "You're very ready."

Grey groaned. *"Yes."*

She carefully drew her hand away. His hardness stood out from his nest of salt-n-pepper grey pubic hair. Too firm a touch and she could hurt him or set off an orgasm that would eliminate the need for the condom she held. Too light and the condom might tear going on or fall off as they coupled. She curled her fingers and thumb into a circle. She moved her fingers and thumb apart as she raised her hand until she could see Grey's cock. Down and over him, she slowly lowered her hand. Grey jerked his hips up off the bed, thrusting him through and against her palm and fingers. On his next move, she closed her fingers around him, lowering her arm as he lay back.

"Much more of that and I am gonna blow, love." Grey held his hand out, palm up. "Maybe I should put the condom on."

Amie laid the condom on Grey's palm. "I'll hold you so you can get it on quicker."

Grey nodded, positioned the condom between his finger and thumb, and eased the condom down and over his sensitive cock. As his hand met Amie's, she let go and rolled away from him.

"On our sides, spooning, is one of my fondest memories of our love making." Amie turned on her side with her back to him.

Grey closed the space between them until he pressed against Amie, her arse and legs tight to his crotch and cock. Amie lifted her leg. He scooted down, placing his hand on her hip and rocked forward, her hand closed around him again guiding him into her. Warmth, not scalding hot warmth, mellow warmth cascaded over him as if welcoming him home. Inviting him to come in and stay. Find pleasure and relax. Orgasming wasn't relaxing to some people. Slow and steady, Grey began working his hips back and forth. In, pause, and let things soak for a moment and the slow retreat back to the start. Amie picked up his rhythm mimicking his moves in with her counter moves.

"Oh, darlin'. This is so good," he managed to get out as he started to pick up the pace. "How you doing?"

"Not far behind you." Amie rolled her nipple between her thumb and finger, pulling it as she stroked up and down her clit with one finger, then two. Short fast strokes, pausing long enough to coat her fingertips with her wetness.

She matched Grey's thrusts until she felt him thrust in and grip her waist tight. She rubbed her clit faster, tightened her muscles around Grey and rocked back toward him quickly.

"Yesss," Grey groaned.

"Oh, me too," Amie moaned. Her eyes closed. Bursts of color, images from the past of trips together, Grey holding her and shared passionate kisses flashed across her vision. The last image was of them snuggled together on a friend's couch.

Several moments of quiet passed. Amie wasn't sure when she returned to earth. Her jumbled thoughts kept one central item up, she'd come home. Found a place where she'd longed for, wished for and knew in her heart—deep in her peaceful heart was the right place.

Grey started to pull away from her. He yawned twice. "Be back in a moment." Amie rolled on to her stomach, pulling the blanket and sheet over her. She watched Grey walk into the bathroom. She blinked twice, yawned, and fluffed her pillow. Grey crawled back in bed, cuddling up to her as he smoothed the sheet and blanket over both of them.

Grey kissed the top of her head and murmured 'good night'. Amie smiled, turned slightly, and said, "Ready to try living with you again."

*Seven hours later*

Grey rolled over, squinted, and inhaled. He glanced at the nightstand clock. Eight-thirty A.M. Dreams vivid and surreal had danced behind his closed eyes until his bladder nudged him into a semi-coherent state four hours ago. Amie had scooted past him about the same time. Falling back to sleep cuddled together had ignited more dreams and thoughts about the last words he thought he heard Amie say. Another chance at living together. Another chance at them as a couple. Could they get it right this time? Images flashed through his dreams like an old film until his dizzy psyche screamed enough. He'd awaken to the quiet moments when dawn and the night whisper their hellos and good-byes. Streams of early morning sunlight created a variegated mosaic pattern as he padded across the chilled floor two hours ago. He'd finally slept without dreams or thoughts. Somewhere in the still quiet, he'd found peace. Peace in making no plans. No expectations. Questions raced through his mind as he glanced at Amie. She stirred, opened her eyes, smiled, and snuggled closer.

His breathing deepened as his eyes closed. Peace, quiet and the stillness of the moment permeated deeper into him. Amie entwined her fingers with his. Time for questions and talking would come later.

One yip. Then another followed by barks and whines. Grey sighed. So much for going back to sleep with Mick and Pixie awake. "All right you two. We're getting up."

# CHAPTER NINETEEN

More yips and barks sounded. Amie tossed off the covers, sighing. "And people say pets are quieter than kids."

Grey snorted. "Hey our four legged ones slept through the night."

"I think we all conked out about the same time." Amie sat up and stretched.

Grey leaned over, captured her nipple between his lips, worrying it with his teeth.

"Not in front of the children dear. You might give them ideas." Amie cupped her breast, leaning closer to Grey. "Hmm, I like that."

Grey continued suckling for a moment longer. He let go, tipping his head back, his lips puckered.

Amie brushed her lips over his and pulled back. "I call dibs on the shower. I need to wash my hair."

She straddled Grey, rubbing her mons back and forth over his erection.

"Who said we need to protect the kids?" Grey thrust upward.

Amie rocked forward, laying her hands on Grey's chest. One stroke followed by another across her clit. Shivers began deep within her vagina as her clit swelled.

Grey clasped her hips as he spoke. "If we're going to finish this we need another condom."

Amie pressed her lips together. Coitus interruptus...all for a good reason. Her doctor said her chances of getting pregnant were smaller since she started menopause. Getting pregnant this late in life put her and the child at risk. She and Grey had talked about kids early on in their relationship attempts. Both had wanted them. The time and circumstances hadn't mixed to give them a chance to be parents. Maybe there were justifiable reasons. Maybe there weren't. Being the adopted grandparents, aunties, and uncles along with second moms and dads were their open options. She nodded. "You're right."

Grey slid his hands down on to her legs stopping her from moving off him. "You okay?"

"Yeah." Amie took a hold of Grey's wrist. "I better move."

Grey shook his head. Amie's tone sliced into him quicker than if he'd walked across ice in leather-soled shoes. Had he said something wrong? His tone? Word choices? She wouldn't meet his gaze.

He dropped his hands, reached up, cupping Amie's chin, he gently tilted her head back until their eyes met. "Talk to me. What's wrong?"

Amie's chest rose and fell with each breath. She blinked, looked away, and licked her lips. Her bottom lip quivered like a twig buffeted by a strong breeze. Lord, had he misread things again?

"Ever look at the past and wish you'd made better choices?" Amie shrugged. "I need to move."

Grey slid his hands away from Amie. He held them up in between them. "How about lying next to me while we talk?" He patted the space next to him and the blankets.

Amie moved off Grey and into the space, pulling the sheet over her. "I'm not sure I can explain what I'm feeling any differently."

"It's okay. I think I get part of what you're saying. You're wondering why we couldn't get it right before." Grey rolled on his side. "Is that what you're saying?"

"In a way, yes." Amie fluffed her pillow, easing it behind her head. "Sometimes missed opportunity sneaks up and smacks you.

Taunting you with past possibilities and scolding you where you failed."

Grey pulled the sheet over him as he scooted closer to Amie. "Honey, I've done my share of kicking myself about stuff like that too. At some point, you have to let go and move on."

Amie looked at him. Her frown hadn't left. There was no mistaking the teary shine to her eyes. She felt deeply about what they were discussing. This was important. He needed to hear her out.

"Go on and tell me what has you feeling guilty." Grey brushed his lips over Amie's. She looped her arms around his neck.

"Why we haven't worked out before. Where did we fuck up? It had to be more than mess up. What did we do wrong?"

Grey inhaled slowly. As he exhaled, he wondered if either of them could pin point the whys. Was it fear that had Amie asking this or trepidation they were fouling up again? He wet his lips. Time for vulnerability. This was the talk they needed to have seven years ago. The deep heart felt frank disclosure that they'd skirted around and alluded to.

"I can only speak for me." Grey laid his arm on Amie's waist. "A couple of times I was too self-centered. I couldn't admit to myself what I wanted. I kept thinking we wouldn't work out."

"So what makes you think we will now?"

"First, I can't guarantee we will. But. . ." Grey used the corner of the sheet to wipe more tears off Amie's cheeks. "We know where we fouled up in other relationships. We know places we messed up in ours before. This time we're not in a hurry to prove something."

"What if I want to sleep with you instead of my own room?"

"Fine with me. You can have your own room too if you want." Grey brushed his lips over Amie's again. "Nothing says we're joined at the hip. Right now, we're settling in and sharing space. Needs are going to vary. Change will happen and the more we openly discuss it. . ."

"I agree," Amie said, sitting up. "Honest open communication and respect are very important to me."

Grey nodded as he tossed off the sheet. "Same here. It's not easy at first to be frank, open, and honest. I think though we're off to a good start."

Amie took a deep breath held it, wrapped her arms tightly around herself and let go a deep pent-up sigh. "After getting burned with my last two attempts at relationships, I'm skittish. Sometimes doubts rear up and coldcock me good."

She chafed her arms as she continued to speak. "I'm owning my fears and caution."

Grey sat up, held his arms apart, grinning. "Darlin' been there a few times myself. Probably will again. I'm offering a warm hug and a chaste kiss. Ask for these any time you need them."

Amie smiled and leaned into Grey's embrace. "Thank you. I'm offering you the same. This is one of the strong reasons I value our friendship and maybe now the addition is us as a couple. You give awesome hugs and know how to read me."

Grey waited until Amie laid her head against his chest before he rolled his eyes. Knew how to read her? Not as well as she thought. He wasn't going to burst her bubble. He wasn't going to lie to himself either. Taking a risky shot in assuming what was wrong wasn't what he was going to do any more. A tenet his last session with his shrink encouraged him to embrace had echoed through his mind more than once last night and this morning. Ask questions. Paraphrase, hear each other out, and make safe space to openly talk about your problems and expectations. He'd done part of that. Now if his blasted cock would stop thinking each time Amie brushed against him it was a signal to repeat last night they might get out of bed and on with the day.

He kissed the top of Amie's head. "You called dibs on the shower. Go on. Take one and get warm. I'll let Mick and Pixie out."

Amie scrambled out of his embraced, kissed his cheek, and dashed toward the bathroom. "Thanks Grey. You're awesome and loveable."

Grey kept a firm grip on his tongue between his teeth. Each of them had used the L word at one point during their recent conversations. He was pretty sure where his had gone, been, and was. Blurting it out without examining his feelings and understanding where Amie was coming from wouldn't solve a damn thing. Might even upset the foundation they built up. He opened the closet and took his robe off the hook on the back of the door. As he put it on, he noticed his hands weren't sweaty, no knots in his gut or a lingering splash of trepidation remained. Perhaps the road map he'd always relied on before and the plans that so often went helter-skelter due to a single sided steering committee, aka him, wasn't at the helm. He and Amie were a team and each doing the driving.

He slipped his feet into his slipper moccasins, let Mick and Pixie out of the crate and exited the bedroom. As he sauntered down the hall following their four legged kids, he grinned more and began whistling an old sea jaunty his great grandfather taught him. Life and relationships were looking up.

# CHAPTER TWENTY

Grey opened the blind covering the patio door. He reached for the handle, stopped, glanced from side to side, and let out a low soft whistle. Snow covered parts of the patio and grass. The sun peeked out from behind the clouds briefly, shining brightly against small drifts toward the back of the yard. He shielded his eyes with one hand as he unlocked the sliding door close to the kitchen. The snow was a quarter way up the six-foot high fence surrounding his yard. He looked out across the yard wondering if he should let Mick and Pixie out without their coats. As he started to turn, wind swooped over and across the top of the fence sending snow scattering in different directions. Mick whimpered and pawed at the door. His sign he needed to go out. Pixie stood behind him, her tail wagging. She walked up to the door and sniffed. Her tail stopped wagging and she started to squat.

"Hold on Pixie," Grey said, sliding the door open enough for Mick to squeeze by Pixie and out the door. Pixie followed him. Another blast of wind rattled the fence, sending snow flying straight toward Grey and the door. He slid the door closed as the snow pelted against the glass.

He stuck out his tongue, blew a raspberry, and glanced over his shoulder. Good, Amie wasn't behind him. Giving into his childlike need to make faces at snow and antagonize Mother Nature was one of the few things percolating through his mind. One main percolation was coffee.

"Damn that wind is cold." Grey checked where Mick and Pixie were in the yard before entering the kitchen. They hadn't ventured far from the door. Mick stood sideways, his leg lifted and his head ducked. Grey shook his head. At least Mick wasn't peeing into the wind. Pixie was close by, partially squatted with her hind legs and feet in the air helping her avoid the wet cold snow. Grey knew he had a very few minutes until they would want back in. He didn't blame them.

He filled the coffee maker's water reservoir, added three scoops of coffee to the drip basket, and pushed the start button. Last night Amie had mentioned helping him make breakfast. He opened the refrigerator door and sighed. He needed to grocery shop. They carton of half-n-half they'd bought along with the cinnamon rolls, a quart of orange juice and a week old half dozen of eggs graced the top and second shelf. He might have a few slices of cheese left in one of the lower drawers along with a couple slices of ham. Makings for some sort of omelet. Sweet rolls, juice, coffee, and the omelet would get them fed. There still was the grocery run he needed to make. Grey pulled a pen and writing tablet out of the drawer closest to him and tossed them on the counter. As soon as he opened the patio door, Mick would make a beeline for his bowl. Probably with Pixie right behind him.

Priorities—feed two cold possibly snowy wet dogs, pour a half cup of coffee, and get fully awake. Sipping coffee strolling down the hall planning his day might not be his first action, though it usually was. His morning routine certainly was starting out different. Changing one moment at a time, one-step at a time. First step was to feed their two noisy four legged kids barking outside the patio door.

"Quiet you don't get," Grey muttered, sliding open the patio door. Mick and Pixie squeezed through the small opening before he could get the door more. Right behind them trying to sneak in with them came a blur of snow and icy wind. Grey slid the patio door shut with a thud. He stuck his tongue out at the snow battering the glass. As he turned, Mick and Pixie watched him, their heads moving back and forth almost as if their puzzled question echoed out.

Grey snorted, shook his head, and walked back into the kitchen. Thank goodness, Amie hadn't heard or seen any of this. Moments like this were better kept between him, Mick and Pixie. Not that they would ever let his secret out.

He opened the cabinet below the counter, took out two cans, glancing over his shoulder. Mick stood at the edge of the kitchen entrance, his tail wagging so fast his hiney appeared to vibrate. Grey swore Mick had an alternative power source going on. If he could only find a way to harness it. Pixie yipped and trotted part way into the kitchen. Her tail wagging some.

Grey chuckled. "Okay you two. Breakfast it is." He filled each of their dishes and set them on the floor close to where they had fed them last night as dinner cooked. Mick sniffed his bowl, then Pixie's. He took two bites, sneezed, shook his head, and went back to his bowl. Pixie didn't sneeze. She tasted Mick's food and went on about eating hers.

"Coffee, shower then dress." Grey filled his mug half way. Two spoons of sugar and a dash of cream slowly stirred into the hot brew later, he lifted the mug to his lips, blew, and sipped. He leaned against the counter, savoring the warmth and sweetness sliding over his taste buds. Did he wait until Amie came out of the bedroom to go take his shower? Or would she welcome his assistance showering like last night?

Amie exited the shower. Heat hadn't changed where her thoughts fixated. Wrapping the towel tightly around her, she slowly inhaled, knowing her stubborn psyche wasn't going to let go of its persistent jab. She needed to talk about something that had bothered her for years. One of the many things she wished they'd talked about the first time they tried getting back together. How would Grey take her need to talk about kids? She wasn't pining for them. Her miscarriage hadn't soured her on enjoying other people's children. Her pregnancy hadn't survived past the fourth month. Grey never knew about this. Truth was she didn't know if she'd gotten pregnant on her one nightstand with Grey or another guy she'd been dating. It was time to share this secret. Time to let go and heal. Time to stop letting her past own a large chunk of her perception of herself.

She unwrapped the towel, dried her hair, and hung the towel up. No more hiding. No more lying and stifling her feelings. She wasn't escaping. Liberation was her destination and it wasn't far away.

Bits and pieces of where to start the conversation formed and died as she put on her panties and bra. Words failed to form that easily broke the ice about what she needed to say. As hard as it had been to put write her feelings out during her grieving, she'd burned that journal entry. Burned it on her California beach camping trip six years ago. She remembered most of what she'd written on the tear stained page. Her pain came out as jagged and torn like the edges of the sheet she'd written upon.

Amie pulled on her jeans and sweatshirt. Combing her fingers through her hair, she nodded. Yes, telling Grey mattered. Better he find out now than to hear it from someone else. She trusted him in many ways. It was time to trust him with this.

Grey slowly opened the bedroom door. Was that a sob? Amie was crying? He set his mug on the nightstand. "Amie, are you okay?"

She nodded, but didn't look at him. "Yeah, I'm fine."

Grey watched and waited, counting to five before he...fuck with waiting. Amie was upset. He wasn't waiting for her to tell him she was okay again. She'd wiped her eyes twice. The tissues on the bed signaled this louder than if she'd yelled it out. Something was wrong.

He sat down on the bed next to Amie, slid his arm around her waist, and hugged her tight to him. "Talk to me, please. What's up?'

"I-I I'm fine." Amie leaned into him and sighed.

"No you're not. Last time you were like this is when you found out your grandmother passed." Grey cupped Amie's chin, tilted her head back, brushed his lips over her cheek. "Did you get bad news? You can tell me. I'm here for you no matter what."

Amie faced him, tears streaming down her face and whispered. "Even if I miscarried your child?"

# CHAPTER TWENTY-ONE

Grey hugged Amie tighter to him. Words...emptiness filled his mind. Shock—dismay—perhaps even anger. . .yet none of this described his state of being. He opened his mouth to speak and quickly closed it. Actions were needed. Consoling Amie mattered more than his gut bouncing up and down like a toddler on a trampoline gleefully giggling. Except his was gut wrenchingly giggling with insanity. His heart pounded, slowed, and pounded again. There was no formulated way to handle what Amie had said.

His brief experience with miscarriages came from his cousin's experience. Henry and his wife Tara had waited and wanted children for the better part of their marriage. Ten years in, they'd given up hope of having their own and set about adopting. Three weeks before their final court appearance, Tara woke up ill. As the day progressed, blood and cramps followed until the emergency room and ambulance happened. Henry damn near lost his wife. Tara almost bled to death. Thank Deity, that hadn't happened to Amie.

Hers had hit her hard. Real hard. Worse than a sucker punch in his gut. He took a deep breath, exhaled, and wet his lips.

"I'm sorry," he murmured. "Why hadn't you told me before?"

Amie sniffled and scooted away from him. "I didn't know how. I grieved. And grieved more. You were the one person I dreamt of having children with. We shared so many talks about this."

He held out his hand. "I remember. We talked about if a pregnancy happened early out in our first time together. Your smile.

100

Your eyes glowed as you talked about wanting to be a mother. I even glowed too thinking you were the one I wanted to have kids with. The mother of my children."

"Yeah." Amie clasped his hand. "I wasn't sure I was pregnant. My periods have always been wacky. Sometimes I'd skip a month even on the pill. Three months in and the pregnancy test pink line told me."

Grey blinked twice. His eyes watered and he knew why. Sadness...for opportunities lost, not being there for Amie and for her having to bear this all alone. "When did this happen?"

"Six years ago. After our one night stand. We'd talked about getting back together..." Amie's voice trailed off.

"All I can say again is I'm sorry. I took a leap at a job offer in Memphis, figured I'd call you once I got settled and well. . .I fucked up royally. Too focused on me and finding out I lost the job six weeks in. Moving back home with my parents even for a month wasn't easy. I still should have reached out, called..." He shrugged. "Go ahead cuss me out. I'm guilty."

Amie patted his hand. "I could have reached out too. Especially after my gynecologist confirmed the miscarriage. The time in the hospital wasn't too bad. My aunt came and stayed with me until I was on my feet."

"Is there more you need to tell me? Talk about?" Grey let go of Amie's hand and moved closer to her. Touching her mattered, reassuring her and letting her know she still had a place to call home here with him even if she wanted to be roommates only.

Amie exhaled a deep sigh. "Are you angry? We missed the opportunity to have kids together. I chose to not attempt that with others. The miscarriage caught me by surprise. I've let it hold me hostage until now. Telling you matters. Do you still want to live together?"

Grey leaned close to her and whispered, "Yes, I do. I better understand why you insisted on condoms. I'm open to talking about having kids."

She cupped Grey's cheek. "Thanks. I'm not sure being a mom and dad at our age is an option. Health is a major concern. My gynecologist took me off the pill last year since I'm premenopausal."

"I wish you had told me sooner. I'm sorry you had to go through this alone. I can't make it up to you. I want you to know no matter what I am here for you. You matter." Grey turned his head and kissed her palm.

"Thank you." Amie cupped Grey's face between both hands, rested her forehead against his. "I don't expect you to make it up or even hold you responsible. Neither of us is to blame. I kept it quiet because I didn't want you thinking I was trying to tie you to me."

Grey slipped his arms around her waist, hugged her tight to him. "It doesn't make it any easier knowing that such things are normal. I'm glad you trust me enough to tell me."

Amie nodded. "Me too. If you have more questions, I'm open to talking about it at another point."

A loud growl and gurgle sounded. Grey pulled back, looked down, and grinned. "I think we've been out voted. Your stomach says food."

Amie smiled. "Yeah, I did say I'd help with breakfast."

Grey lowered his arms. "Coffee is made. Mick and Pixie fed. It's cold out. Snowed some last night. Let me grab a shower and I'll help with breakfast too."

Amie stood, stretched, and gathered up the used tissues. "I'd like to promise you something."

"What?" Grey took off his robe. Tossing it on the bed, he started toward the bathroom.

"If we need to have more of these kind of conversations, I'll do my best to be present in the moment and not stuck in my own recriminations." Amie kissed Grey and moved around the foot of the bed.

"Honey, I'm sure we'll have more discussions. Some hard, some easy. And probably a few heated arguments too. I believe we've got a stronger bond and foundation because we're best friends and know each other as well as we do. Trust is a key element in all of that."

"True. Very true." Her stomach growled again. "I'm going to get some coffee and a yogurt. We'll figure out the main course when you're ready."

"Sounds good. Be ready soon." Grey entered the bathroom, closing the door partway.

Amie tossed the tissues into the wastebasket near the bedroom door. Trust. . .she finally had the word. That along with a very special feeling that set her heart to fluttering, and her thoughts soaring. There was a hint of the L word too in their communications. Were they ready to say it? Acknowledge it?

She flexed her hands, inhaled and exhaled twice, and exited the bedroom. Whatever happened going forward, she'd won her freedom. Doubts and uncertainty would rise again. They shared a past. A rocky one mixed with glorious moments of passion, unity, and the L word. Damn, she still censored her thoughts and her verbalized self-talk. Maybe that was the other so-called pebble in her shoe. She almost told Grey she loved him two years ago as they embraced farewell at the end of that year's Valentine's lunch. Was he ready to hear her say it? Was she ready to hear her say it? To say it out loud? She wasn't sure. Part way to the kitchen, her stomach growled again. Amie smiled. "Yes, food and coffee. Doubt sneaks in when the mind and body are focused elsewhere."

Grey stood under the spray of hot water for several moments. He closed his eyes, fixated on his heartbeat as he slowly inhaled, held his breath, and exhaled. Every time his mind diverted from this, he repeated the exercise. Through soaping down, rinsing, and washing his hair. Ten minutes of forced focused meditation. The one tool he'd mastered early out in his sessions with his shrink. Being in the moment, the here and now instead of getting swallowed up in his fear, disdain and allowing his doubt to drive. Amie trusted him enough to tell him about her miscarriage. He learned another thing since last night, he wanted her around. He listened and heard her. Confirmed as they talked what she said. They were communicating. Could their hearts speak as clearly?

Grey dried off quickly. He tossed jeans, a long sleeved t-shirt and briefs on the bed. He yawned twice as he reached for his cup of cold coffee. Vagueness, fear, and doubt were not going to drive him and Amie apart this time. The slow steady lub of his heart echoed his thoughts. They were ready to be a couple again. How did he explain this? That was going to take actions and words. He had one down. The other he wasn't so sure about.

He took a sip of cold coffee. "Ain't no way in hell that is going to help format coherent words!"

He set the mug down, raced around the bed, hastily pulled on his clothes, socks, and hikers. He needed hot coffee and food before he started formulating anything.

# CHAPTER TWENTY-TWO

Amie gripped her coffee mug with both hands and lifted it. Tendrils of heat rose, aromatic scents of fresh dripped coffee greeted her as she brought the cup to her lips and sipped. A dash of cream, three teaspoons of sugar, and a huge mug of caffeine awaited her as she sipped more. She set the mug back on the counter. Pixie and Mick had greeted her as she reached the kitchen. Their whimpers and scratches at the patio door said what they wanted and needed.

The two culprits stood near the door after she got them outside. They kept looking back at her like they needed instructions on what they were out there for. Bless Pixie's dislike for cold and snow, she'd run out into the yard a bit farther and squatted. Her hind end up in the air and her back feet almost level with it. Mick squatted not far from the patio door and left his pile. Pixie practically bowled Mick over in her rush to get back to the door.

Amie opened the patio door. "All right. Had enough outside, did you?"

Wind rushed in behind Mick. Snow followed closely behind in an orderly fashion as it swooped off the fence and fell in to line behind the Mick, Pixie, and the wind. Amie jumped to one side, quickly sliding the door closed. "February and the blasted ground hog says an early spring. No way that varmint is correct!"

Mick and Pixie dashed by her. Where they were making a beeline for she could almost guess. Either the couch or the bed. She took off at a trot behind them. "Mick," she called out. "Pixie. Sit."

"I'm ahead of them," Grey answered. "Brought their rug out and put it on the couch. Bedroom door is closed."

"Thanks." Amie reached for the coffee mug Grey carried. "More coffee?"

"Yes. Dump that out and fresh from the pot please." Grey let go of the mug. "I hate cold coffee."

"Yes, but we drink it any way if needed. Like commuting to work." Amy rinsed Grey's mug out and refilled it from the pot. "Pot is almost empty. Shall I brew another one?"

"This one is fine for me. You going to want more?"

Amie set Grey's mug on the counter, lifted her mug, and saluted him. "No, I found the mug you put out. Enough for two cups. Thanks."

Grey chuckled. "See I remembered. You weren't sure last night I would."

Amie gulped another swallow of coffee from her mug. "Well it's been a while since you and I faced a morning wake up together."

"Yeah, a couple of years at least. Some family get together I think." Grey creamed and sugared his coffee. He took two sips and set his mug down. He faced her.

"Probably Sheila's wedding. You needed a date and so did I. We went stag thinking we could slip out. HA!" Amie opened the refrigerator door. "Not much in here for breakfast fixings."

"Sheila's mom thought she could work her wiles on me and get back us together. I learned the hard way with that one to stay clear and out of sight as much as possible." Grey reached into the refrigerator. "Omelets, cinnamon rolls, and coffee. I might try one of your yogurts. Haven't found a fruited one I like yet."

"I'll make the cinnamon rolls. You do the eggs?" Amie took the roll of crescent rolls from Grey. "Help yourself to a yogurt."

"Sure, I'll do the eggs. There's a couple slices of cheese and some ham I can dice up and add to the omelets." Grey stepped past her carrying the egg carton. "Do you mind making out the list? Your handwriting is better than mine."

"That's an understatement. I write like a doctor, remember?" Amie set the oven to preheat and popped open the crescent roll tube. "Baking sheet?"

"Pizza pans in lower bottom drawer to left of refrigerator. Simple easy multiuse cooking utensils and pans." Grey set a skillet on the stove.

*Ring...Ring...Ring.* Grey pulled his cell phone out of his jeans pocket. Glancing at the caller id, he grimaced. "Shit, I gotta take this call. It's a client I've been trying to reach all week. I won't be long."

Grey waited until he was in the hall heading to his office before he answered the phone. "Hey Jack. Thanks for returning my call."

"Sorry Grey to catch you on a Saturday. But it's the first time I've had open all week." Jack's voice cut in and out.

"Jack, you're cutting in and out. Where are you?" Grey sat down at his desk. He pulled a pad to him and grabbed a pen.

"I'm in between flights. I've been in Los Angeles all week. Contract negotiations with one of my major suppliers. I'll be in Memphis next week. Can you meet with me there?" Static crackled like Jack's call dropped.

Grey hastily scribbled notes as he spoke. "Probably. How long will you be in town?"

"Grey are you still there?" Jack asked and quickly added. "In Memphis for two weeks. Board of directors is meeting. They want to go over your presentation. I think you got the contract."

"Let me call you tomorrow. I'll know more then. Thanks for letting me know." Grey waited for Jack's answer. Nothing but more static. A few minutes later, his phone buzzed. He looked down. A text from Jack read. "On plane. Call me Sunday evening around seven. Talk more then."

Grey pumped one then two fists in the air. Opening his own accounting firm was finally paying off. Jack's Rib Joint and Bar was expanding and they needed a head accountant. One that Jack trusted. Grey hoped the board of directors would too.

He pushed back from his desk and stood. He'd text Jack later. The flight would probably take four to five hours. Grey exited his office, carrying the pad he'd made notes on. Would Amie want to go with him or be okay moving in without his help? There was furniture, belongings and her car to move. He might be able to leave midweek and come back the following Monday. Driving to Memphis would take about three hours, maybe less depending on traffic. There'd be time to talk as they ate.

Grey sniffed as he got near the kitchen. Cinnamon and bread smells teased him and fled. He inhaled the closer he got to the kitchen. Fresh baked bread and cinnamon greeted him along with sounds of sizzling and popping. "Man, those rolls smell good."

Amie leaned over and kissed his cheek as he got close to the stove. "Rolls are done. I started the omelets. How'd your call go?"

"Good. I'll explain while we eat. I'm going to make up the list." Grey tossed the pad he carried on the table. "What do you eat for breakfast each morning?"

Amie chortled. "Whatever is simple and easy. Usually a bagel and a hardboiled egg and a mug of coffee."

"Okay. Eggs, bagels and more coffee. How about cream cheese or butter?"

"Either. Depends on what's on sale that week." Amie placed one omelet on a plate. She set the skillet back on the burner and poured the remaining egg, ham, and cheese mixture into the pan. "Let's make up the list while we eat."

"Sure. Do you want yogurt with your meal?" Grey opened the refrigerator. "I'd like to try the tart cherry one."

"I want the peach melba." Amie flipped the last omelet out of the pan on to the empty plate. "How did your phone call go?"

Grey picked up his coffee mug, moved to the table and sat down. "Well, it's hard to say. You've heard me talk about Jack Roberts and his restaurant."

Amie put the pan in the sink, filled it with water, and carried the two plates to the table. "Your fraternity brother if I remember correctly."

"Yes. And my first client when I opened my own accounting firm two years ago." Grey took a plate from her. "You did better than I could have."

Amie smiled as she sat down. "Thanks. I mixed the cheese and ham into the egg mix and folded the mixture in half as it cooked."

"The art of taking time to prep things instead of quick and easy. I've got to remember to take time for that. Too much fast cooking and eating while working at same time." Grey picked up his fork. "Jack incorporated six months ago and I'm presenting why I should be the corporation's accountant at the next board of directors meeting."

Amie stopped chewing, looked at Grey, waiting for him to continue. He grinned and began eating his omelet. She shrugged, finished chewing, and swallowed. She sipped her coffee and filled her fork again. She took a bite as Grey spoke. "The meeting is sometime within the next two weeks in Memphis."

# CHAPTER TWENTY-THREE

Amie grabbed her napkin and praying she didn't spit food all over before she could cover her mouth. She pressed her lips together, hoping she didn't bite her tongue as she did. She stopped chewing, swallowed as best she could and laid her napkin down. She laid her hands on the table, leaned forward, and asked. "It's when?"

"Within the next two weeks." Grey held up his hand. "I know it's a surprise. I didn't know either until I talked to Jack."

Amie leaned back in her chair, relaxed her hands, and nodded. "Well, I guess I best stop unpacking and get Pixie and I ready to go back home."

"You are home." Grey laid his fork down. "Nothing's changed about you and me. You're welcome here. As far as I'm concerned your home is here."

"Right. How am I supposed to get all my stuff moved? We'd talked about making some decorating changes. At least for my room." Amie continued eating.

"Get all your stuff moved? This is news." Grey stirred his open yogurt with a spoon. "Looks like we've both sprung surprises on each other."

"Could be." Amie looked up and back down at her plate. She kept eating though part of her wanted to toss her fork down and go pack.

*Stop acting thinking like a pained child*, her conscience chastised.

Truth was sometimes a bitter mouthful. Especially when it was truth she was wrong. Grey hadn't said more than the meeting he

110

needed to attend was sometime in the next two weeks. She'd jumped to conclusions. Spilled her heart's unspoken desire. Laid it all out and surprised herself more than anything else.

"Care to elaborate?" Grey asked, sipping more coffee.

"I surprised me too. I'd given totally moving in some thought while showering." She opened her yogurt and stirred it. "Are you sure moving in while you're out of town is okay?"

Grey smiled and nodded. "It's fine. How about you move in smaller things like your clothes and Pixie's things? Then when I get back, we move in the rest. All the big stuff."

"And decorating?"

He took a deep breath, waited as he listened to his heart's steady beat and noted his lack of sweaty palms. "I have three things. No print wallpaper. No neon colored clashing accent painted walls. Third, if you're unsure, just ask. I trust you. You're a crafter, an artist of sorts and a bit of interior decorator."

"You trust me implicitly?" Amie put the empty yogurt carton on her plate along with her fork and spoon.

Grey pushed back from the table, stood and reached for his plate. Did he absolutely trust her? Completely trust himself to not trip himself and fall back into his own fear. The fear that kept replaying the botched decorating jobs housemates and college roommates sprung on him or even Sheila's mom with the chartreuse and olive colored walls in their bedroom. Trust had to grow more. Begin showing up and being shown in actions and words. His palms were sweaty. The hair on the back of his neck stood up like it was at attention and his stomach...well it just gurgled and sent smoke signals to his brain about cinnamon rolls slathered with butter. "I must," he began, knowing the chasm before him required a leap of faith. Faith that he didn't know where it came from. May be it was trusting him to know what he really wanted. And that was Amie here. Here at home with him. More than that he couldn't verbalize if he needed too.

He licked his lips and continued. "I absolutely trust you to make good choices, good decisions and talk things out when you're in doubt."

He picked up his plate with both hands, hoping he didn't drop anything from them shaking like a 5.0 on the Richter scale earthquake. He'd just opened his life and home in a way he hadn't expected too. What the future held remained to be seen?

"Thank you. I agree with you. I ask the same of you." Amie pulled the pad to her. "I'll print the list out. I write in short hand quick and choppy otherwise."

Grey smiled. "I scribble in acronyms and a few words. Guess both of us has internalized our jobs."

Amie picked up the pen. "This might be why we've had ups and downs in our recent conversations. We're listening but not really listening."

Grey put his plate in the sink and walked back to the table. "I suspect—No I know I wasn't focused completely all the time. I let my subconscious jump to conclusions and accepted them as what was happening."

Amie handed him her plate and mug. "I'm guilty of the same. Before you leave for Memphis I'd like to have some heart to heart hearing each other focus discussions."

Grey brushed his lips over Amie's. "I concur. We've got to set a strong foundation. It may take more than just a couple of conversations."

"It might. For now, let's get this grocery list made." Amie printed three items on the list. "I've got milk, eggs, and meat. What else?"

Grey rattled off several more items as he rinsed the dishes and placed them in the dishwasher. "What about Pixie and Mick supplies?"

Amie nodded. "Yeah, tomorrow we can get some stuff boxed up to bring over and more of Pixie's stuff."

Grey leaned down and hugged Amie. "I'm glad we had this talk. The more we focus on the here and now the better we communicate."

Amie patted his hand. "There's truth in that. How soon you want to go to the store?"

"I'm ready now. You?" Grey turned the dishwasher on.

"Let's round up our four legged kids and go." Amie tore the list off the pad and pushed back from the table. "Want to take them with us?"

"Nah, its cold out there and they would fuss being in the car. I don't think we need to crate them."

Amie stood. "I'll get my coat and purse. Meet you in the living room."

Grey tore a sheet off the pad and wrote three items on it. He'd made a simple dinner for Amie in the past she raved over. Tonight he wanted to show her through words and actions she'd come home.

Grey gripped the steering wheel harder. "Either some idiot retimed all the lights again or everybody thinks it's a great time to be out and about."

"Better to take it easy and get to the store safely." Amie patted his leg. "Besides, we can talk about paint colors for the living room while we wait."

Grey snickered and snorted. "A loaded question for sure. Loaded with lots of color, I bet." He glanced at Amie.

"Sure why not. After all there are lots of other colors than white, beige, or eggshell." Amie grinned and added. "I promise no neon colors or glow in the dark stuff."

"Okay, seriously what color would you suggest? I've thought about an accent wall behind the TV and perhaps doing the hallway in another complimenting color." Grey put on the left turn signal.

"Do you want pops of color or solid color in each room?" Amie asked.

He glanced at Amie as he moved into the left most lane of the two turn lanes. "As beautiful as rainbows are, I don't want one inside my house."

Amie chortled. "You don't mind color, complementary colors. Just don't put them all together in one room or one wall."

"Hey, our great minds think alike." Grey pulled into a parking space close to the market entrance.

"Could be." Amie leaned over and kissed his cheek. "I also remember the day-glow colors our neighbors in one apartment chose. I don't know whose head ached worse at the end of helping them paint their place. Yours or mine."

"Mike and Cindy were great people. Their color choices needed a dimmer switch for sure." Grey unfastened his seatbelt and opened his door. "Who gets to push the cart?"

"We can take turns." Amie got out and shut the passenger door. "My days of climbing in and out of the cart stopped by sixth grade."

"Mine stopped earlier. Around eleven. Mom sent me along with dad to make sure he stuck to the list. His impulse buying was awful." Grey pulled a cart out of the line close to the entrance. "Liver and onions. The house reeked when he got done cooking."

"No wonder you looked at me like I lost it the first time I offered you pate." Amie put her purse in the cart's toddler seat.

"Yeah. My grandmother would profusely apologize when I called asking if I could stay with her for a few days. My answer to why was the *air* needed to clear! *Literally!*" Grey followed Amie into the market.

# CHAPTER TWENTY-FOUR

Amie pressed her lips firmly together, trying to contain her mirth. Poor Grey. He'd talked about his dad's cooking fiascos off and on during the times they lived together. Grey had learned how to cook for his own defense and his grandmother feeling he needed to know how to survive. Or as Grey put beat dad to the kitchen with easy to cook recipes. She enjoyed several of his meals when they first started dating. She hoped he would make some of those meals again. Especially her favorite—Southwestern Chicken Sauté with Broccoli. Just enough heat to sizzle her taste buds and zing to take two cold beers to cool down.

She turned; ready to ask Grey about his plans for tonight's dinner. He stood off to a side, looking intently at his phone. She turned around and started back toward him.

Grey looked up. Amie had gone on ahead thinking he followed her. His phone had buzzed twice before he got out of his jacket pocket. Jack's last batch of texts finally came through. He wasn't meeting with the board of directors until Wednesday. The earliest they wanted to meet about the accounting presentation and contract talks would be toward the end of the week. That might give him and Amie more time together before he drove to Memphis.

"Hey sorry. Phone buzzed back-to-back. Thought it might be important." Grey put his phone back in his jacket pocket.

"Was it?" Amie turned the cart so she stood close to him.

"Jack's texts finally came through. He's meeting with the board on Wednesday. They might meet with me later in the week." Grey pulled the list out of his jeans pocket and smoothed it out.

"Sounds good. Let's get shopping. More people just came in. Looks like everyone is making a run before or after a storm."

"You'd think we were going to get snowed in." Grey pointed to the aisle closest to them. "Let's start there."

"Okay. I don't remember putting any international food items on the list." Amie reached for a jar of jasmine rice.

"I didn't say we needed rice either." Grey took the jar from her and put it in the cart.

"You don't have any. I checked and you asked if I still had the recipe for my sweet jasmine rice pudding."

"I did. I appreciate you remembering. What else do you need for the recipe?" Grey picked up a bottle of southwest blended spices and a jar of salsa.

"Condensed milk, raisins, and cinnamon. You going to make your southwest chicken sauté?" Amie placed his items in the cart next to the rice.

"The first time I asked you to stay for the weekend; I welcomed you with a meal and invited you to make my home your home." Grey added two more items to the cart.

"Yes, you did. I remember that night, the food, your arms around me as we slow danced in the small open area close to your couch. That studio apartment saw us through good and bad times our first year together." Amie entwined her fingers with his.

"It's like we're at the first time again. Yet we're not. We're wiser, more experienced—at some things." Grey paused.

Amie grinned and nodded.

Grey continued as he raised Amie's hand to his lips. "Other things we'll learn along the way. We've already started with our communication. We're taking time to talk and act together." He brushed his lips across her knuckles and let go.

"Oh wow Grey. I think you just told me all over again from last night up to now you're welcoming me home. Inviting me in, in to stay in so many ways." Amie slipped her arm around his waist, hugged him, and brushed her lips over his.

"Yes I am. And now to answer your question, I'm gonna make Southwest Chicken Sauté tonight with some of your jasmine rice and broccoli." Grey grabbed a bag of tortilla chips off the end cap of the chip and soda aisle as they passed it. He placed them in the cart. "My turn to push."

Amie moved away from the cart, holding her hand out. "Have you marked off the list what we got?"

Grey snorted. "No, but I can. Do you have a pen? I forgot to grab the one off the table."

Amie unzipped the front pocket of her purse and pulled out a pen. "Can't say I'm always prepared. Mostly prepared is a better description."

Grey took the pen from her, glanced at the list and line off several items. "Okay, we still need breakfast and other lunch items. How about grilled cheese or your grilled tuna patties on rye?"

"Sounds good. You get the soups. I'll get the cheese and tuna. We'll meet back at the butcher counter in say about ten minutes?"

Grey nodded and took off at a trot, pushing the cart. Two aisles over he turned down the aisle, stopping midway down it. He grabbed two cans of chicken noodle soup, a package of stew starter, and a large can of minestrone. If he remembered his grandmother's enhanced recipe right, a half-pound of ground beef and a can of spicy tomato paste would kick the soup up a notch with enough zing to warm and sizzle taste buds. As he exited the aisle, he added two boxes of assorted crackers to the cart. Cheese and crackers appetizers would complement the soup. The next aisle held an assortment of beers and wines. As he glanced up the aisle, he caught Amie pausing at the end of it.

"Meet in the middle?" he called out, going down the aisle.

"Sure." Amie met him almost mid aisle close to the beer cold case. "Mexican for the Sauté? Ooh, minestrone. That calls for wine or an American brew."

"American? Minestrone is Italian." Grey put a six-pack of Mexican light beer in the cart.

"Yes, but if you are making your grandmother's Americanized version. It needs the hardiness of an American brew." Amie held up a local indie brewed beer in Nashville. "How about this?"

"Different. Let's try it." Grey set the six-pack in the cart next to the other beer. "Let's get the rest of what we need and get out of here."

Fifteen minutes later, they approached the checkout area. Two pounds of ground chuck, four rib eye steaks, spaghetti fixings, dog treats, and dog food rounded out the purchase. Grey helped the bagger pack items. Between the canned vegetables, packs of cheese and lunchmeat along with the four pack of tuna, lunch, and dinner were covered. The last three bags held their breakfast makings. English muffins, loaf of rye bread, butter, eggs and a bag of hash browns.

Grey pushed the cart the back of the car. He brushed bits of snow off the trunk before opening it. More snow had fallen as they shopped. The wind wasn't as sharp and cold. More sun beamed through the broken clouds. The afternoon would warm up some more. He doubted much of the snow would melt before nightfall. "Looks like winter is trying one last round. How about a fire in the fire place tonight?"

Amie picked up a bag from the cart and put it in the trunk. "Sounds good. Is there a hardware store near here?"

"Might be. " Grey set two bags in next to the others Amie had put in the trunk. "Why?"

"Paint chips. Color guides. You know things that spark more conversation about there not being a rainbow in your house. At least *not* as the main theme in your living room or maybe your bedroom." Amie grinned and blew him a kiss as she put the last bag in the trunk and closed it.

Grey smirked, turned the cart around, and walked back to the cart return. He gripped the handle of the cart tightly before he shoved it back into the return. He inhaled slowly and let go of the handle. Exhaling, he noted his palms weren't sweaty. His heart wasn't racing. Maybe his earlier statements about trusting Amie implicitly was his own pep talk about trusting his gut and heart and letting them lead instead of expecting more of the past. Time to move forward into the here and now was happening.

Amie stood outside the car watching him. Was she reading him? Thinking his body language said one thing when it wasn't? Grey wet his lips and said, "Sure. Let's go see what they have. We can discuss what colors might go where tonight as we eat dinner. I'm open to *us* making the house *our* home."

Amie didn't say anything. She nodded and got in the car. What had just happened? He couldn't stand there dumbfounded. Could he? To say not much took him by surprise was an understatement. 'Cuz Amie had taken him by surprise.

# CHAPTER TWENTY-FIVE

Grey shook his head and snorted. Talk about scoring and possibly without a plan. Amie had a high five coming for sure. Well, maybe a silent one he'd acknowledge for now. He opened the car door, got in, and started the car.

He glanced at Amie. She kept looking straight ahead. He could assume he oopsed, ask if he oopsed, or just keep his mouth shut. This was the stop assuming action his shrink had chastised him about more than once. The outcome was sometimes risk came with finding out what you needed to know.

He turned in the seat. "Did I say something wrong?"

Amie looked at him. A smile on her face. "No. I was at a loss for words. We've had good communication. Moved another step closer in actively hearing each other and not second guess."

Grey held his hand out. Amie laid her hand on his. He closed his fingers around Amie's hand as he spoke. "Created safe space to speak up, know we heard each other, and clarify as needed. Good for us."

"Yup. We paraphrased too. Kinda of scary also." Amie squeezed his hand and pulled hers away. "Sweaty palms and cold car makes me chilly."

He turned the heat on. "Sorry. Now, Rayburn Hardware is at the opposite end of the shopping plaza. The paint area is upfront. You still want to go check out what they have?"

Amie nodded, chafing her hands together. "Yes. A couple of main color books and paint chip samples is all we need. If we decide we don't like those we can always come back."

"True. You look for paint chip samples. I'll get the color books. Sam Rayburn is one of my client's." Grey parked the car close to the entrance.

"Are you sure it's a good idea to..." Amie's voice trailed off.

"A good idea to what?" Grey unfastened his seatbelt.

"Well mix business and pleasure, I guess." Amie grinned and shrugged.

Grey chortled. "If buying paint is a pleasure, when did I miss this new description?"

"I suppose it's no different than me sending one of my clients to the yarn wholesaler across town. We send each other business. Buy from each other." Amie opened the passenger door.

"Your businesses are similar. Sam's and mine are two distinct separate businesses. I still don't get how buying paint is pleasurable." Grey got out of the car. "Please explain."

Amie pressed her lips together. Color, creativity and the action of putting the two together was as natural to her as breathing, taking a patient's temperature and recording their vitals. She turned, glanced at the sky, and pointed. "See how the clouds frame the sun. It's a sight that has many unique aspects. You see it one way. I see it another. I like decorating working with colors, textures and creating a special feeling."

Grey moved up to the front of the car, holding out his hand. "You mean like when we took that pottery class and created those vases for our moms."

Amie clapped her hand over her mouth. Images of two lopsided badly painted with garish colors vases flashed through her mind. Lowering her hand, she took a hold of his. "Not that bad. Remember we got better as the class went along."

"You got better. I transferred to the photography class. At least I learned about photo layouts and some marketing ideas from the professor and his wife who taught the class." Grey stepped up on to the sidewalk in front of Rayburn's.

"I know the color basics I've considered." Grey held one hand up. "Yes, other colors than white, beige, or eggshell. I'll grab those books."

"All right. I'll get the accent color paint chip samples." Amie winked. "I promise no rainbows on the wall, but..."

Grey smirked. "Rainbow colors are permissible as accents." He kissed Amie's cheek and pulled Rayburn's door open. Dinner discussion was going to be lively.

Sam greeted them shortly after they entered. Business was slow. Sam laughed at Amie's suggestion about painting each room a color from the rainbow. Grey shook his finger at her and continued looking at the mix of blues, teals and tans paint color books Sam handed to him. Twenty minutes later, Grey and Amie waved good-bye to Sam as they drove off.

"You sweet talked Sam." Grey glanced at Amie. "His grandmother loves to cross stitch. That pattern you looked up for him and got express shipping at a discount on, won him over."

Amie nodded. "That pattern is one that my great aunt did during the summers she taught me about cross-stitching. Being able to pass the joy along to another is worth the time and energy it took me to locate it."

"Thank you. Sam also wanted to know if you were seeing anyone. I asked him why. He said you were a gem worth keeping." Grey eased into the traffic on Main Street.

"What did you tell him?" Amie turned in her seat, facing him.

"I said I didn't think you were available. If you were interested you'd let him know." Grey slowed for the stop light close to their next turn.

Amie laid her hand on his leg. "I thought you said Sam was married."

"He is. He told me I needed to declare my intentions." Grey turned in the driveway.

'He told me the same thing. He said if you were willing to let me decorate, I must be pretty special. I thanked him for his observation and would think about it." Amie got out of the car.

Grey unlocked the trunk, picked up two bags, and stepped in front of Amie. "I told him about the same thing. It's good to know what we've got is strong."

"Indeed. I'm glad we're building on the solid foundation we've had for quite a while. Best friends and lovers who understand each other pretty damn good."

"I agree. Let's get these groceries put away. Mick and Pixie out for another potty break. Then we can start discussing dinner and potential painting." Grey unlocked the front door. "I'm eager to try the decorating websites Sam told us about. See what colors might look like without paint splotches all over the walls."

"That is going to be fun. I get to paint a rainbow on your pretend wall. Then maybe you'll agree having one on an actual wall won't be so bad." Amie trotted past him into the house.

Grey chuckled. The next few hours were going to be a mix between artistic, chaotic, and unique. He hoped artistic and unique came out on top instead of chaos. He didn't want a repeat of the chartreuse and neon orange tied-dyed paint patterns like his and Amie's first decorating project had turned out. That damn paint had glowed in the dark. Even a dimmer switch couldn't have helped that bad paint job.

Grey yawned and stretched. Amie lay with her head in his lap, partially asleep. He glanced at his watch. Where had the day gone?

Mick and Pixie found one of the neighborhood cats' dead mice in a corner of the back yard. The two had dug up and rolled in the decomposing corpses until they reeked more than a bag cut onion stashed in a week old bag of garbage. Between the dirt and stench, bathing two dogs who all of a sudden hated water created a mess on par with Mick and Pixie's prebath status.

Dinner had prep and cooking took longer than expected thanks to doggy bath time. He and Amie had worked side-by-side, laughing, joking, and sharing memories. Throughout dinner, they'd discussed colors, pro and cons of certain mixes along with their personal preferences. On the coffee table lay two lists. The one closest to him read potential colors. The other, forget it colors. The website Sam directed them to, helped to a point. Color combinations still needed working out. Tomorrow was the end of the weekend. In short, amount of time they'd spent together, they'd bonded in ways he hadn't expected. The surprise of the evening was Amie sweet whisper to him before she started to doze. "Grey Dunstan I think I'm falling in love with you again."

He hadn't answered. Only cupped Amie's face between his hands and passionately kissed her. In their younger days, the trashcan would have several used condoms in it and the scent of their mating permeating the air as they fell asleep. Right now, he wanted to cuddle Amie close to him, savor the few hours they had left before the workweek intruded. One other good thing was Jack texting that the board meeting was set for Thursday. A few more days with Amie and getting used to coming home to her was a wondrous gift, he loved having.

# CHAPTER TWENTY-SIX

Amie slit open the box of embroidery thread and laid several bags on the counter. She started laying each bag of color out, checking them against the packing list. After several moments, she laid the packing list aside. She walked into the back room. Four days prior, Grey had kissed her goodbye, told her he loved having her sharing the house with him, making it their home. He'd promised to call when he reached Memphis. The call had turned into a text. Five hours lapsed before Grey answered. Last night's call was brief. What was supposed to be an easy meeting had turned into a major power struggle between Jack and the board of directors. Grey was in more meetings than he anticipated and wasn't sure when he'd be back.

Charlotte and Roberta had helped her box up the last of her clothes along with her kitchenware. Ten more boxes sat in the backseat and the trunk of her car ready to take back to her and Grey's place. She'd still referred to the house as Grey's more often than she liked. Charlotte teased her about surrendering her independence. Amie knew better. She'd surrendered to what her heart and psyche knew. She'd fallen deeper in love with Grey. In love with the man, she knew for many years. Stood shoulder to shoulder with her frequently throughout their friendship as it matured into best friends with occasional benefits and into now...

"How do I describe us?" Amie poured a cup of herbal tea from the pot she brewed earlier.

"Describe who?" Charlotte asked.

"Sneaking up on me?" Amie asked, turning around and entering the shop.

"Might be. You never know what good gossip you may miss if you don't." Charlotte laid her jacket and purse on the counter. "Got another cup? That smells divine."

"It's a new mint medley from the new tea and coffee shop over on Bristol." Amie handed Charlotte her cup. "Here I can get another."

"Thanks. I came by to see if you wanted to have lunch." Charlotte sipped some of the tea. "You're right. This is quite good."

"Be back in a moment." Amie walked back into the makeshift storage room office area and poured another cup of tea. She cupped her hands around the mug and inhaled. Fragrant peppermint mixed with spearmint and wintergreen scents brushed against each nostril, teasing her to sip the savory blend. Grey was supposed to call tonight and confirm when he'd be home.

"Hey you get lost back there? You okay?" Charlotte called out.

Amie rolled her shoulders, inhaled and exhaled. Doubt and worry were taking their toll on her. Her psyche kept comparing things to prior incidents, trying to put the past on the same level as current things. Grey had explained briefly what was going on. In the past, he hadn't always. She hadn't asked either. Shying away from discussing hard topics hadn't worked out then. She needed to know more of what was going on. Partnering meant taking an interest in each other's jobs and understanding how they affected each other.

"I'm okay. Lost in my thoughts. Four days ago, Grey kissed me goodbye and said I'll call you love." Amie faced Charlotte. "He's called me love and sweetheart more and more."

Charlotte set her tea mug on the counter and dragged one of the client stools behind the counter. "Sit. You look like you're about to cry. Why?"

"I'm not sad. Confused. Fearful and perhaps a bit of apprehension." Amie sat down. "Grab another stool so we both can sit."

Charlotte dragged a second stool behind the counter and sat down. "Drink your tea. I've got something to say."

Amie nodded and sipped her tea.

Charlotte picked up her mug and held it out in front of her. "You're scared. Not because you're sure things won't work out. You're unsure they will work out. Who was it that told me to stop fearing change and make a leap of faith aka trust my heart and gut?"

Amie set her mug down. "I did. So did several others. You'd been trying to retire for four years. Even talked about opening the shop. Asked me to be your partner."

"That's right. I kept waiting for the perfect time. The perfect amount of money and the perfect spot. I thought everything had to be perfect. All lined up to take that next step. Well I faced my fears and got to the core of the issue."

"Which was?" Amie asked.

"I didn't trust me. Trust that I knew what needed done. I had tried to open a business in the past. Failed or so I thought. Instead, I learned I made my first attempt in learning." Charlotte drank more of her tea. "The more I let go of expecting perfection and embraced learning while prioritizing checking in with me, the further ahead I got. Make sense?"

"Are you saying I don't trust me?" Amie finished her tea. "Or I don't trust Grey?"

"Maybe both. Trusting isn't easy. It is easy. It depends on what your view is. Are you seeing who you are now? Who Grey is now? Or are you stuck in the past more than in the here and now?" Charlotte set her empty tea mug next to Amie's.

"Damn how is it you can read me so well?" Amie smirked.

"Because you've told me more than once no one else matched up to Grey." Charlotte laid her hand on Amie's arm. "I think you never stopped loving him. Your heart and head warred over what was best. Have you told Grey about how you feel?"

"I tried to over the years. I guess I wasn't ready to admit I still cared that much. Possibly even scared to say let's try again when we botched up getting back together a few times," Amie said.

"Did you ever say hey Grey what happened? Why?" Charlotte patted her arm. "Don't kick yourself over it. Hamish and I tried to reconcile before our divorce was final. We couldn't see past our pain, anger, and fear. A couple years ago, Hamish remarried. His wife and I are good friends."

"Sounds like Grey and I becoming best friends and staying connected. We're closer than we realize." Amie picked up the empty tea mugs. "Lunch offer still open?"

"Sure. I'll let you in on something Grey told me a last fall." Charlotte put her jacket on.

"What?" Amie asked, heading toward the kitchen area in the storeroom.

"He hit the jack pot with you. He knew he had a good thing and you were the one." Charlotte picked her purse up off the counter. "I told him tell you that. Talk about what he wanted."

"Why did he tell you this?" Amie called out.

"He wasn't sure how to tell you. He came to me for suggestions. Like I could advise him on what to say." Charlotte slung her purse over her shoulder. "Rascals has their chili salad on special. Let's go there."

"Well you did in a way tell Grey what to say." Amie grabbed her jacket off the coat rack close to the office door and put it on. "Yeah, Rascals sounds good. I'm glad you didn't tell me about this until now. I'm not sure I would've believed Grey then like I do now."

Charlotte walked to the shop door and turned. "What changed?"

"I started trusting me. Learned to listen to myself and figure out what I wanted and want. I want Grey. I've fallen in love with him again and again. This time I'm ready to say it out loud and own it." Amie reached up, flipped the open sign over to out to lunch. "And make it work. Do the hard work and keep on believing and trusting in Grey and me."

"Good for you, honey. I'm happy for you." Charlotte followed her out the door. "Tell Grey when he gets back."

"I'm going to tell him when he calls tonight. I think we're ready to admit what we want. We're ready to love each other again." Amie pulled her sunglasses out of her purse and put them on. Letting Grey know was one thing. Was he ready to tell her what his heart was telling him?

# CHAPTER TWENTY-SEVEN

"Sorry, Grey. I didn't know Terrence Withers…" Jack stopped speaking. "Hell, I offered him a partnership when I first opened the bar and bistro. He turned me down flat."

Grey set his half-empty beer bottle on the bar. "Sit down Jack. It's not your fault. Even if you knew, Terrence was going to try a force takeover. You couldn't predict when he would do it."

"Yeah, it unnerves me. The board split on the vote and now I'm back to a sole proprietorship. And to spread shit even more Terrence tried to call me about buying in." Jack grabbed his beer and guzzled half of it. He set the bottle on the bar and dropped on to the stool next to Grey. "What the hell do I do now?"

"Take a deep breath, shred lots of paper and get glad. You don't have to file incorporation papers. Saved those fees. And got yourself an attorney and an accountant." Grey picked up his burger and bit into it.

"Thanks for sticking by me. I appreciate it. You're a good friend." Jack took a bite of his burger.

Grey wiped his mouth. "You're welcome. You stuck with me when I opened my business. First few years weren't easy."

Jack laughed. "Oh, do we know. Well the bistro is turning a regular profit. The bar is gaining ground. So what's next for you?"

"Me?" Grey swallowed more of his beer. "What do you mean?"

"You mentioned Amie a couple of times when you first got here. We haven't had much time to talk. Are you back together?" Jack took two bites of his burger, motioning for Grey to talk as he did.

130

"Depends on how you define back together." Grey popped the last of his burger into his mouth and slowly chewed.

He and Amie back together. He mulled the thought over and over the last few days. He fell asleep thinking about her. She crossed his mind often during the day. Even doodled her name on his notepad more than once during the meetings. Oh, he had it good. His heart and conscience nudged him harder the last few days. He'd fallen in love—make that fallen deeper in love. How that came to pass he wasn't sure. Somewhere in the middle of last night as he lay awake letting his thought wander, he found understanding. He'd never fallen out of love with Amie. He thought they wanted different things. Parted due to needing space. Way things were going before he made the trip to Memphis; they'd both previously screwed up.

"I think it depends on how you define back together." Jack said wiping his hands on his napkin. "If you and Amie say you're back together, then you are."

Grey nodded. "Very true. Our friendship is a cornerstone of why we've remained connected. I'm finding out I should have done the opposite of what I thought was right in our earlier break ups."

"What's the old saying about hind sight being perfect and foresight mono-focused?" Jack picked up their plates and walked behind the bar. "Are you doing better knowing this?"

"Don't know. It's more like we're actually listening to each other. Asking questions and checking in. Except. . ." Grey pointed to the pitcher setting on the bar. "We're waiting for the shoe to drop."

"You don't know what the other is going to say and you're afraid to look inside?" Jack set two glasses on the bar and filled them with water from the pitcher. He handed one to Grey.

"Might be. I suspect Amie and I are tiptoeing around wanting certainty. I've said there isn't any." Grey drank some of the water and set the glass down. "I don't want to hurt her. I don't want to hurt me."

Jack came around the bar, held up his palm to Grey. "High five on figuring out life and loving someone. We don't want to hurt them or us. Life and love come with risks. We know this."

Grey high fived Jack back and sat on a bar stool close to him. "We sure do. You and Nancy have twenty-five years together and twenty of those married. Amie and I have almost as many but the opposite of yours."

"So, do you take the risk and tell her what's in your heart? What's been there all along from what you're telling me? Or do you keep quiet?" Jack guzzled his glass of water and set the empty glass on the bar. He reached out and touched Grey close to his heart. "I think you already know the answer here."

Grey nodded. "I probably do. It's time to tune into me and figure out what I need to say."

"Be safe, my friend. There's a cab waiting to take you back to the hotel." Jack embraced him in a strong hug.

Grey hugged Jack back and stepped away. "Thanks for the food. Thanks for listening."

"Any time. Our friendship goes beyond business." Jack handed him his jacket. "One more piece of advice. Call Amie and talk with her. It's okay to talk about business and include her in what's going on."

Grey pulled on his jacket and zipped it. "I will. Her last email and text about painting both bathrooms bright yellow and orange needs a verbal answer for sure."

Jack shook his head and burst out laughing. "At least it ain't that damn tie-dye shit you did in your first place together. Looking at those pictures made my eyes hurt."

Grey laughed as he opened the door. "You only had to deal with pictures. *We lived in that fiasco for three years!*"

Jack stood in the door as Grey exited. "Well you only have to look at yellow and orange bathrooms a few times a day."

Grey pressed his lips together trying to control his mirth. He shook a finger at Jack, exhaled, and said, "I'll send you several pictures so you can look at the paint job. Get your sunglasses ready if that is what we decide."

Grey got in the cab, waved to Jack, and leaned back against the seat. He glanced at his watch. 4:45 P.M. Damn the day had flown by. The morning meeting had turned into a shouting match twenty minutes in. Terrence and his cohorts had walked out as the shouting subsided. Jack had offered those present the opportunity to leave or vote to adjourn after deciding if they wanted to invest in the bistro and bar. Grey rubbed his hands down his pants. Some had hemmed and hawed. A few spoke up stating their confidence in what Jack proposed.

In some ways, his and Amie's recent discussions were similar. Avoiding the topics and some they spoke about their confidence in each other. Did that extend to them as a couple? Were they ready to let go of the past? Maybe they had in bits and pieces.

Jack was spot on about making the leap, trusting what his heart and gut kept telling him. Repeatedly telling him for over a year. He hadn't stopped loving Amie. He'd fallen deeper in love with her in a way that he hadn't realized until now. Did he tell her over the phone or in person?

Grey got out of the cab, paid the driver, and entered the hotel. If he left right now, he might get home around ten or eleven depending on traffic. He yawned twice as he crossed the lobby. Inside the elevator, he yawned again. Heading out in the morning after a relaxing evening and a good night's sleep made sense. Amie would understand. He'd call her after he napped.

# CHAPTER TWENTY-EIGHT

Amie settled back against the couch. Her empty dinner plate set on the coffee table. Pixie and Mick snoozed on the couch next to her. 7:00 P.M. She still hadn't heard from Grey since earlier in the day when he texted he'd just gotten out of the last shit storm board meeting. Granted she'd worked most of the day covering for Roberta who asked for the day off to attend her latest granddaughter's christening. Amie picked up the remote, clicked through several channels, and shut the T.V. off. Nothing interested her. Her latest cross-stitch project sat on the end table where she put it right before dinner. On the floor next to the rocker she'd purchased two days ago sat the bag of yarn and crochet pattern she wanted to work on as a gift for Roberta's new granddaughter. Distraction wasn't going to fill the need, the want, nor the desire to hear from Grey.

She tossed the remote on the coffee table, rose, and picked up her dishes. Mick raised his head, wagged his tail, and sacked back out. Amie smiled. Pixie was out cold. Both of them had run from one end of the yard to the other chasing each other for almost twenty-minutes when she let them outside as she prepared dinner. Pixie ate, hopped up on the couch, turned around twice close to the pillow on Grey's side of the couch, and flopped down. Mick had followed suit. Amie wished she could sleep as sound. Last night she drifted off after exchanging a couple of text with Grey. Somewhere near dawn, she awoke and couldn't go back to sleep. Hugging his pillow, inhaling his scent or rereading his text messages over the last few days hadn't calmed her enough for deep sleep.

"Damn it, Grey. I need to hear your voice. I want more than a few lines on a screen." Amie walked into the kitchen and put her plate in the sink. Cooking for one wasn't fun anymore. She sighed. Tossed back her head, and voiced her angst. "I don't want to be constantly alone. I'm ready for us to be together. More together than we got before you left."

She gripped the edge of the counter tighter. Did she sound clingy or needy? Maybe both. Damn, why did communication have to be so hard?

*Why didn't you ask for what you need? her psyche chastised her.*

"What I need is different than what I want. I need Grey here. I want to know what is going on. I can't just say Grey I want you to come home." Amie turned around, leaned on the counter, and closed her eyes. Blurting out things worked to a point. If she could phrase it in a different way. Interpreting her own needs at the same time she tried to balance Grey's—"It's not easy."

She chuckled at the image flashing through her mind. Grey hog tied to a chair and gagged. The next frame showed her tied up and gagged while Grey spoke. Keeping their attention focused on what the other was saying instead of leaping a head or assuming mattered. Maybe this was why she didn't like blathering about what her needs and wants were. She needed input.

*Input comes from talking to Grey, her psyche added.*

"That's for sure." Amie turned back to the sink, opened the cabinet close to her, and took out a wine glass. She set it on the counter and opened the refrigerator. The bottle of wine she'd bought on her way home sat on the first shelf where she left it after she uncorked it last night. She took the bottle out, uncorked it again, and filled the wine glass a quarter full. As she set the bottle back in the refrigerator, a hum and buzzing sound coming from the front room caught her attention. She'd left her cell phone on the coffee table.

She quickened her pace as the buzzing sounded again. She glanced at the caller id as she picked up the phone. Grey was calling.

"Hey handsome," she said, perching on the edge of the couch arm. "You're wonderfully alive. Talk to me."

Grey's chuckle warmed her ear and heart. Hearing his breathy laughter said more than his response did. He was happily calling her. He wanted to talk and hear her voice. She focused on what Grey said as he repeated his greeting. "Yes, fully alive now that I hear your voice. Miss me, sweetie?"

Amie weighed her response. Her psyche pricked her, reminding her about asking for what she needed. "Yes, I miss you. So does Mick and Pixie. I want to hear about what's going on with you and Jack's meeting."

"I'll give you the short version for now. I'll need your help sorting things out once I get home. I've got lots of notes."

"Sure. Happy to help. What is the short story tale?" Amie rose and walked into the kitchen. She picked her glass of wine up and sat down at the table.

"One of Jack's supposed staunch supporters tried to stage a coup, a hostile takeover. It blew up and half of the board walked out with Terrence when Jack told him to shovel his shit elsewhere. The remaining members voted to buy in as limited partners. When Terrence heard what happened, he tried to make peace and offer to buy in for a full partnership. End of tale is Jack is a sole proprietor for now and has an attorney who is backing him on things. What's up with you?"

Amie sipped her wine and put the cell phone on speaker. "Well no orange and yellow pictures to send you yet."

Grey's snort and laugh rumbled out of the phone. "Thanks for waiting for my help on that move. I think we could come up with a better color combination if you're still serious about a beach affect in the bathrooms."

"That is an idea I hadn't thought about. An oasis. Maybe a spa getaway. Hmmm. Well remodeling isn't in this budget." Amie tittered. "You can breathe Grey that never came to mind."

"Thank you. At some point, we might. Not right now," Grey said. "Mind if I change the subject?"

Why did Grey want to change the subject? Had she...damn it, she wasn't going to cower. The past was done. Over, gone and couldn't be changed. It was time to let it go and move into the here and now.

"Depends on what the topic is." Amie sipped more of her wine. She covered her mouth, hoping she muffled her yawn. Hearing Grey's voice soothed her. Relaxed her in a way she hadn't anticipated. They were talking. Too detailed or too deep and she'd not make sense. She needed sleep. Sleep would come when the call was over.

"How do you feel about us?" Grey didn't say more.

"Uh. I think we're gonna be fine as housemates. We're doing good so far." Amie looked at her nearly empty wine glass. She'd smothered two more yawns before Grey asked his question. Now she was awake. Her heart pounded. Sweat slicked her palms.

"That's great. I'm asking how do *you* feel about us." Grey's emphasis on *you* left no room for supposition. What did she say now? Be vulnerable and say what her heart whispered multiple times during their weekend together? Say the L word and take a risk? Would the risk be any less if she said it in person? What made the difference? She didn't know. Grey hadn't said more. She needed to answer him. He deserved a reply.

Amie licked her lips, wiped her hands across her jeans, and rose. She picked up her phone and wine glass. She walked into the kitchen as she spoke. "Grey, I'm solid on us. I know we've got something good going. I'm comfortable being around you and having you around. I like what we're building."

"Good stuff, love. I'll be home midday. I'm looking forward to sleeping next to you tomorrow night. I've been lonely. You've got a large chunk of my heart. Good night, darling."

"Good night Grey. You've got a huge part of my heart too." Amie ended the call. They hadn't said the L word. They'd come close. Waltzed right up to the edge of admitting they'd moved beyond best friends with benefits. Could they say the word face-to-face? Tomorrow might be the time to do it.

She put her glass in the sink, shut off the kitchen light, and went back to the living room. She petted Mick and Pixie rousing them enough to follow her into the bedroom. As she undressed and got ready for bed, Amie kept focus on one thing Grey said, he looked forward to sleeping with her because he was lonely. A small spark flickered and grew as she closed her eyes and sleep claimed her. What would tomorrow reveal?

# CHAPTER TWENTY-NINE

Grey turned up the radio volume. The easy rock station somehow had captured his mood. Focused on Amie, what his heart and gut kept pumping through him with every love song. Oh, he had it. Had it good. There was nothing bad about cherishing someone, caring deeply for them, and—"I might as well admit and say it. I love you Amie."

Somewhere in his ponderings as he drove home, he hit upon the one thought that eluded him for almost a month. His heart whispered it in his dreams, his faint visions down memory lane, and presently as he acknowledged what he felt now. He understood he'd felt it all along. He'd never quit loving Amie. The degree and intensity shifted a bit. Being in love still mattered. The teenage angst had its sweet spot in their early years. As they matured, it took the steps life experience and understanding brought to change his in love notions. His notions had taken on a robust acceptance and depth that remained steadfast. "Yeah, I learned to control me better and to let go more. Be realistic in what I want and figuring out how to work as a team."

Grey chuckled at the image going through his psyche. Amie and him at. . .

He slammed on the brakes, skidding to a stop. Cars filled all four lanes in front of him. Everything was at a total stand still. "Shit!" he muttered, reaching for his cell phone. The radio station's traffic alert signal sounded.

"Traffic update on Route 22. Inbound toward Peyton Corners, there's a three-car pileup thanks to a flock of determined geese and a stubborn jackass. No, my good listeners I don't mean a bullheaded fool, human or animal. Whole Grains Farm fence came down last night and their donkey pair, Tilly and Mel, decided to have an adventure. Problem is Mel is sitting on his arse in the middle of Route 22. Stay tuned for more updates in ten minutes."

Grey let go of his cell phone, reached up, and wiped his eyes. The harder he pressed his lips together, the more he snickered and snorted. Talk about a bop on the head from deity. He'd been as stubborn as Mel a few times. Maybe one day Mel would get the message. Grey knew he had. Stubbornness only got you so far. Listening and communicating opened up more doors or illuminated other paths. He looked up, gave a thumb up, and said, "Okay, I got the message loud and clear. Thank you."

Traffic started moving very slowly, inching up the road. The station's traffic alert chime sounded.

"All right folks. Reports are Mel saw the error of his way and moved. The geese mess is almost cleaned up. No fatalities, except a few feathers and bird manure. Tow trucks are on the scene. No humans were hurt. About another twenty minutes and traffic should begin to clear."

Grey pulled on to the shoulder and reached for his cell phone. It buzzed and hummed twice as he picked it up. Missed call ID showed Jack's attorney's name, Ed Swisher. Grey noted the voice mail icon showing. He'd check Ed's message when he got home. Right now, he needed to hear Amie's voice and let her know about the delay.

Amie picked up on the second ring. "Hey Grey. Where are you?"

"Route 22, stuck in traffic. Mel and Tilly escaped again."

Amie's giggle reached out of the phone, caressed, and warmed his ear. "Those two getting out is a better signal spring is coming than the blasted rodent Phil."

"That is for sure." Grey glanced at his watch. 12:15 P.M. "I'm going to be another twenty to forty minutes before I get to the Main Street exit. I'll be home soon, love."

"Sounds good. Traffic is light in town. I met Charlotte and Roberta for breakfast. I'll be here, watching and waiting for you, dear." Amie waited until Grey hung up before she did.

Last night she'd slept deep, dreamed a lot and woke up twice. In those moments, her thoughts wondered. She tucked them away until this morning, over her second cup of coffee, she wrote them down. When she first met Grey, she was jaded. Didn't trust many people. Grey's college roommate introduced them on a family trip to Myrtle Beach. Everyone pretty much left her alone except Grey. He sat with her, talked about life, and told dumb jokes. She'd laughed and smiled more each times he sought her out. She felt connected to him then. The next time she'd run into him was at a mutual friend's wedding. They'd paired up and spent the better part of the following week renewing their connection and the start of a relationship. Falling for a guy her height, with hair longer than hers was unique to quote her mother. Her father shook his head and walked away each time she said Grey was the one. So many times, Grey had been there for her, partnered with her, been a friend, confidante and a lover. What they had grew and strengthened without either of them realizing it until they decided to be a couple. Somewhere in the middle of all the ups and downs, they bonded in a special way. They became best friends. Break ups and distance couldn't change the connection, foundation, and strength of them. Now, she understood. It was time to tell Grey how she felt. Say the L word, confess it, and glow as she told him.

Charlotte and Roberta offered their advice. Keep cool, cook a nice meal, and be prepared for silence. Amie hadn't told either of them that quiet might not be an option. She and Grey had a lot to talk about. Should she for grins and giggles paint a couple of orange swipes on the wall? Not that she would, orange paint was hell to cover. She swore the paint chip sample Sam had given them glowed in the dark. She wasn't repeating three months of that. Black out curtains and soft glow night-lights hadn't tone that crap down. Four coats of primer and sleeping with the windows cracked in forty-degree weather taught her to think twice with impulse painting.

Amie entered the kitchen and opened the refrigerator. She reached for the bowl containing the pork chops she put to marinate this morning. Grey liked the tart and tang of barbecue sauce mixed with chipotle seasoning. The chops had very little fat and no center bone. It wouldn't take long to bake them. She turned the chops over pushing them down into the sauce and set the bowl back in the refrigerator. As she washed her hands, she checked the list she'd taped to the door with tonight's dinner ingredients. Red wine, bottle open and breathing on the counter, tossed salad in the covered bowl on the third shelf of the refrigerator, her homemade Italian dressing—contents ready to mix right before dinner, mashed potatoes—warmed in the microwave, yeast rolls—what a mess that had made making them from scratch. For dessert, chocolate cake topped with strawberries and whipped cream.

She looked at the pad on the counter with various calligraphy styles she tried practicing in hopes of piping her special message for Grey on the cake. The best looking ones were the block capital letters that spelled the message out clear and easy to read, *I love you, Grey*.

She glanced at her watch. Grey would be home in forty minutes.

Grey eased into the left turn lane close to home. Getting off Route 22 had taken longer than he expected. Once he got on Hazelwood Way, he'd made up time. Soon he'd be home. Back with Amie, Mick and Pixie. The place he wanted to be. Ed's voice mail raised a few questions. Ones he and Amie needed to talk about. Nothing they couldn't decide together. First, he wanted to hold her close and tell her, *I love you, Amie*. The small box in the bag inside his briefcase held a display of his feelings. Deeper than he'd felt for anyone in some time. Did Amie feel the same? What would her answer be?

# CHAPTER THIRTY

Grey listened to Ed's voice mail one more time as he pulled into his driveway. He hoped Amie felt the same way he did after she heard the voice mail and they talked about it.

He paused as he reached the front door, put his key in the lock, and turned it. If Amie had painted the bathrooms orange and yellow, he'd get used to it. This was their home. Together they would decorate it. Determine the esthetic look they wanted. As he entered, he wasn't worried. His gut was calm. His palms dry and his heart beat steady. He opened the door, calling out as he entered. "Hello, I'm home."

Barks and yips sounded. Mick ran up to him, sniffing his shoes and pants. Pixie yipped twice, twirling in circles. As Mick backed off, his tail wagging, Pixie scooted forward sniffing his pants and shoes. Where was Amie? Busy trying to hide her paint surprise?

"Amie, where are you?" Grey set his briefcase and duffle bag on the chair close to the door.

"In the kitchen, love."

Grey paused; she'd said the L word. Warmth surged over him. His heart beat faster. His palm moistened.

"What are you doing?" he asked, inhaling as he entered the kitchen. Fresh baked bread greeted him first. Different cheese scents came next. The last was potatoes. Had she prepared his favorite three-cheese au gratin potato casserole?

Amie turned to him, her hands covered in flour. Her apron had spots and spills on it. As his gaze roved higher, a hundred-watt smile greeted him. Her eyes glowed like happiness and joy filled her. "Welcome home. I'm making dinner. Pork chops with my tangy barbecue sauce. Three chees potato casserole and homemade biscuits. Steamed peas or corn if you want an extra vegetable."

"Sounds wonderful. What a great welcome home." Grey walked over to Amie, leaned in, and kissed her. "Ah love, it's good to be home."

"Dinner will be ready in about twenty minutes. Do you want to talk while I finish prepping the pork chops?" Amie laid her head against his chest, slipped an arm loosely around his waist, and hugged him briefly.

Grey pulled out a chair and started to sit down. Mick and Pixie ran into the kitchen and up to the patio door. They sniffed the door and ran back to where he sat. Mick yipped and went to the door, looking back at him. Pixie lingered part way between the door and where he sat. Grey got up and let them out. Barks and yips sounded as they took off running through the yard. He came back to the table, pulled out the other chair next to him, and patted it. "Come sit down for a moment."

Amie glanced at Grey, down at her sauce-covered hands and back at Grey. The pan with the pork chops sat on the counter ready to go into the oven. Did she finish what she was doing or go sit down with Grey? Grey patted the chair again. She knew what she needed to do. She quickly washed and dried her hands. She turned the chair so she faced Grey and sat down. "I've got a few minutes until I need to put the pork chops in the oven. What's up?"

Grey took a hold of her hand and brushed his lips over her knuckles. He didn't let go as he looked up, smiling. "We've been through a lot together and as friends. You've seen me at my best and at my worst. You moved away and still kept in touch. Each Valentine's Day, we meet up and catch up face to face."

Amie nodded. "You've seen me at my best and worst too. Dried my tears even long distance. Taken my calls at all hours. Valentine's Day is one of my favorite holidays. Favorite because I get to spend it with you." She leaned in and kissed Grey's cheek.

Grey opened his mouth to speak. Loud barks and yips sounded outside the patio door. "Our chaperones are back. I'll let them in. You put the pork chops in the oven. I need to get something out of my briefcase. I'll be back in a few."

"Sure." Amie watched Grey walk out of the kitchen after he let Mick and Pixie in. What was he trying to say? She took a deep breath, exhaled and rose. Panic and fear would have swamped her previously. Tonight they weren't. She and Grey seemed to be on the same wavelength, tuned into each other like never before. Something good was happening. She put the pork chops in the oven and set the timer.

Grey came back into the kitchen, whistling. She recognized the tune from one of the romance movies they'd both enjoyed watching. The two lovers reunited after realizing how right they were for each other. Focusing on the here and now, she understood more of what was happening. Letting go of the past was why she could. Charlotte and Roberta were right. Today mattered. The past was done. The future was theirs to build together if they wanted too.

Grey put a small box on the table and sat down. "Okay. Pixie and Mick are munching on some treats Jack sent back for them. You ready to talk more?"

Amie took off her apron, tossed it on the counter, and sat down next to Grey. "I sure am. What's in the box?"

"You'll find out in a bit." Grey scooted his chair closer, took her hand, and entwined his fingers with hers. "My grandfather passed one piece of advice down to his children and grandchildren. He said never doubt love that keeps coming back, warms you and your heart."

"I like that advice. Good words to live and love by."

Grey cleared his throat and spoke. "Amie, you are the love that warms me and my heart. The love that keeps coming back for me. I love you."

Amie swallowed twice, wet her lips, and held up three fingers. "One-I didn't paint the bathrooms yellow or orange. They're marine blue and beige."

Grey nodded and motioned for her to go on.

"Two-Grey you've warmed my heart since I met you. You are the sunshine that ignites the warmth deep down in my soul and heart. And—three..." Amie rose, let go of Grey's hand, and sat on his lap, looping her arms around his shoulders. "I love you. Always loved you. Still love you."

Grey cupped her face, kissed her cheeks and lips. "I love having you here close and cuddled up. I can't show you what's in the box this way."

Amie grinned as she stood up and winked. "Okay, I'll behave for a while longer."

Grey laughed, picked up the box, and stood. "This is a small token of my love, my desire for us, and I hope our future." Grey went down on one knee as he opened the box. "Amie Ferguson will you marry me? Please continue being the love that keeps coming back and warms me inside and out."

Amie laid her hand on Grey's shoulder. Kneeling in front of him as she did. "Yes, Grey Dunstan, I want to be the love that keeps coming back and warms you inside and out. I want you to be mine too. Yes, I'll marry you."

Grey took the ring out of the box and placed the ring on Amie's finger. "I've got one more thing to ask you." He stood, helping Amie to her feet. "How does being a mom sound?"

Amie coughed twice, opened her mouth, and closed it. She sat down, pointed at Grey and herself. "Wh-what do you mean?"

Grey laid his cell phone on the table. "Jack's attorney, Ed Swisher called me on my way home. Eliza and Zach lost their parents in a car accident four years ago and their grandmother last year. They're too old for foster care at seventeen. Their dad, Jacob, and I worked together right out of college."

"Are you suggesting we adopt them?" Amie rubbed her palms on her jeans. "Aren't we a bit old for this?"

Grey shook his head. "Not adopt them unless they want that. Be foster parents and a place they can call home while they attend college. Eliza and Zach graduated close to the top of their high school class. They've been accepted to some of the top state universities with full ride scholarships. This is our chance to help make a difference in a couple of kids' lives."

The oven timer rang as Amie stood. "We've got the room. Did you know about this when you bought the house?"

"No idea. I hadn't talked to Jacob in years. We lost touch after our second university class reunion. He went overseas and married a woman from England. Ed said Jacob named me as guardian for Eliza and Zach but weren't sure where to find me until Jack introduced us. Are you unsure?"

Amie shut the oven off and took the pork chops out. She set the pan on the top of the stove. "Not unsure. Wanting to get more info before I say yes. Have you met them? Talked with them?"

"Yes right before I left I talked with them briefly. They're willing to give it a try. I'm willing if you are. They're headed to the University of Tennessee at Chattanooga in September. Gives them and us a chance to get acquainted and settle down together." Grey took the plates off the counter and set them on the table along with utensils and napkins.

Amie slipped an arm around Grey's waist, hugged him briefly, and faced him. "It takes a village to raise kids. Eliza and Zach are grown in many ways. Still everyone needs a place to call home. Let's give it a shot and see what happens."

# CHAPTER THIRTY-ONE

*Eight months later*

Grey glanced out across the church pews enjoying the mix of popular and inspirational organ music filling the sanctuary. Today was his and Amie's wedding.

Jack and his wife sat second pew back. Sam and his wife occupied the pew behind them. Roberta and her family sat opposite them on the bride's side of the church. Charlotte and her new boyfriend sat with them. Other friends and assorted family members filled the remaining pews. The officiating minister stood up and moved close to him. Zach stood next to him as his best man.

Zach and Eliza had settled into university life after a few ups and downs. Their grief was healing. They opened up about wanting and needing family to call their own. Talks were underway to settle custody and begin the adoption process. Grey smiled, returning the smiles of those who gaze met his as his met theirs.

The organ music changed heralding of the entrance of the bridal party and the bride. First in were Roberta's grandson as the ring bear and her granddaughter as flower girl tossing flower petals as she walked. Some of them at her brother. Eliza entered next, walking down the aisle wearing a periwinkle blue dress and carrying a small bouquet of white roses and lilacs. The organist played the opening chords of *Marry Me* by Train. The lyrics spoke to both of them. The line about always being happy together and by each other's side brought home what they'd shared, built and the love they'd come to know. Today was the first step in the next phase of their life together. Amie told him last night as he held her she was marrying her best friend and that made her very happy. Grey's smile deepened as the vestibule doors opened again. His best friend stood just outside them ready to make her way up the aisle to him.

Amie entered wearing a pale beige off the shoulder gown. She carried a bouquet of yellow roses and light orange tulips. She inhaled deeply as she made her way up the aisle. The floral mix of the tulips and roses brushed against her nose. Her life had changed and was changing. Valentine's Day marked the beginning of the change. She and Grey had dare to risk, dared to voice their heart's deepest wishes and to hear what they had longed to say again. Their love had grown, deepened, and changed just as their friendship and connection had. From this point forward, she knew she made the right choice in trusting Grey with her heart. As she reached the altar, Grey moved up beside her taking her hand.

"Ready, my best friend?" Grey asked.

"Yes, very ready, my best friend," Amie replied.

The minister spoke briefly on building a life together as partners and friends. Amie smile as Grey repeated his vows. He smiled as she repeated hers. As he leaned in to kiss her, they both whispered, "It's awesome to love you again."

# *THE END*

# About the Author

Solara loves and lives with her partner of 21 years in the Metro DC area. What started out as a bi-coastal romance soon settled on one coast.

A vivid imagination keeps her busy creating her next fascinating romance. She enjoys creating unique characters and watching their journeys unfold. "Love freely given multiplies and will return endlessly" is a key aspect of her stories. Add in alternative lifestyles and her love for the paranormal, and the uncommon becomes the norm in many of her stories.

Her day job in the financial services industry pays the bills while she pens her erotic tales.

Read more at https://solaragordon.com/.